"No need to thank me," Rowdy said.

"You're the one helping me. Saving me from the wrath of Nana is a good thing. If there is one thing she prides above all else, it's that her boys are gentlemen. And I have to admit I have sometimes been her wayward grandson."

Lucy smiled. "I'd hate for you to admit you're helping me remodel my barn because you're a nice guy." And he might be. But that didn't stop her from being wary...not so much of him, but of the way she reacted to him.

"Me a nice guy?" He looked skeptical, and a grin played across his face. "I don't know about that."

The man's personality, like his eyes and his smile, sparkled and drew her in.

Just because she found a man attractive didn't mean she was going to unlock her heart, trust him and eventually marry the man.

He was her neighbor being neighborly. End of story.

Right.

Books by Debra Clopton

Love Inspired

*The Trouble with Lacy Brown
*And Baby Makes Five
*No Place Like Home
*Dream a Little Dream
*Meeting Her Match
*Operation: Married by Christmas
*Next Door Daddy
*Her Baby Dreams
*The Cowboy Takes a Bride
*Texas Ranger Dad
*Small-Town Brides
  "A Mule Hollow Match"
*Lone Star Cinderella
*His Cowgirl Bride

†Her Forever Cowboy
†Cowboy for Keeps
 Yukon Cowboy
†Yuletide Cowboy
*Small-Town Moms
  "A Mother for Mule Hollow"
**Her Rodeo Cowboy
**Her Lone Star Cowboy
**Her Homecoming Cowboy
††Her Unforgettable Cowboy
††Her Unexpected Cowboy

*Mule Hollow
†Men of Mule Hollow
**Mule Hollow Homecoming
††Cowboys of Sunrise Ranch

DEBRA CLOPTON

First published in 2005, Debra Clopton is an award-winning multipublished novelist who has won a Booksellers Best Award, an Inspirational Readers' Choice Award, a Golden Quill, a *Cataromance* Reviewers' Choice Award, *RT Book Reviews* Book of the Year and Harlequin.com's Readers' Choice Award. She was also a 2004 finalist for the prestigious RWA Golden Heart, a triple finalist for the American Christian Fiction Writers Carol Award and most recently a finalist for the 2011 Gayle Wilson Award for Excellence.

Married for twenty-two blessed years to her high school sweetheart, Debra was widowed in 2003. Happily, in 2008, a couple of friends played matchmaker and set her up on a blind date. Instantly hitting it off, they were married in 2010. They live in the country with her husband's two high-school-age sons. Debra has two adult sons, a lovely daughter-in-law and a beautiful granddaughter—life is good! Her greatest awards are her family and spending time with them. You can reach Debra at P.O. Box 1125, Madisonville, TX 77864 or at debraclopton.com.

Her Unexpected Cowboy
Debra Clopton

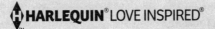

HARLEQUIN® LOVE INSPIRED®

Recycling programs
for this product may
not exist in your area.

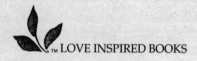 LOVE INSPIRED BOOKS

ISBN-13: 978-0-373-87859-8

HER UNEXPECTED COWBOY

Copyright © 2014 by Debra Clopton

www.Harlequin.com

Printed in U.S.A.

Put your heart right, Job. Reach out to God.... Then face the world again, firm and courageous. Then all your troubles will fade from your memory, like floods that are past and remembered no more.
—*Job* 11:13, 15–16

This book is dedicated to all those making a new, fresh start with their lives. May God bless you and keep you as you make a change in your life.

Chapter One

Rowdy McDermott closed the door of his truck and scanned the ranch house that had seen better days. Carrying the casserole he'd been sent to deliver, he strode toward the rambling, low-slung residence. He'd always liked this old place and the big weathered barn behind it—liked the rustic appearance of the buildings that seemed cut from the hillside sloping down on one side before sweeping wide in a sunny meadow. There was peace here in this valley, and it radiated from it like the glow of the sun bouncing off the distant stream cutting a path across the meadow.

This beautiful three-hundred-acre valley was connected to his family's ranch. Rowdy had hoped one day to make this place his own, but the owner wouldn't sell. Not even when he'd moved to a retirement home several years ago and Rowdy had made him a good offer. He'd told Rowdy he had plans for the place after he died.

Four days ago his "plan" had arrived in the form of the owner's niece, so Rowdy's grandmother had informed him, at the same time she'd volunteered him to be her delivery boy.

He knocked on the green front door, whose paint was peeling with age. Getting no answer, he strode to the back of the house, taking in the overgrown bushes and landscaping as he went. Years of neglect were visible everywhere.

A black Dodge Ram sat in the drive with an enclosed trailer hitched to the back of it. He'd just stepped onto the back porch when a loud banging sound came from the barn, followed by a crash and a high-pitched scream.

Rowdy set the dish on the steps and raced across the yard. The double doors of the barn were open and he skidded through them. A tiny woman clung to the edge of the loft about fifteen feet from the ground.

"Help," she cried, as she lost her grip—

Rushing forward, Rowdy swooped low. "Gotcha," he grunted, catching her just in the nick of time. He managed to stay on his feet as his momentum forced him to plunge forward.

They would have been okay if there hadn't been an obstacle course's worth of stuff scattered on the barn floor.

Rowdy leaped over cans of paint and dodged a wheelbarrow only to trip over a pitchfork— They went flying and landed with a thud on a pile of musty hay.

The woman in his arms landed on top of him, strands of her silky, honey-colored hair splayed across her face.

Not bad. Not bad at all.

She blinked at him through huge protective goggles,

her pale blue eyes wide as she swept the hair away. A piece of hay perched on top of her head like a crown.

"You *saved* me," she gasped, breathing hard. "I can't believe it. Thank you."

"Anytime," Rowdy said with a slow drawl, forcing a grin despite feeling as if he'd just lost a battle with a bronc. The fact that there was a female as cute as this one sitting on his chest numbed the pain substantially.

Those amazing blue eyes widened behind the goggles. "I'm sorry, what am I thinking sitting on you like this?" She scrambled off and knelt beside him. "Can you move? Let me help you up." Without waiting for his reply, she grasped his arm, tugging on him. "That had to have hurt you."

He sat up and rolled his shoulder. "Hitting the ground from the loft would have been a harder fall. What were you doing, anyway?"

Leaning back on her heels, she yanked off the goggles.

Whoa— Rowdy's pulse kicked like a bull as he looked into her sparkling eyes.

"I was knocking a wall out with a sledgehammer. It was a *splendid* feeling—until the main beam gave way and I *flew* over the edge like a ninny." A nice blush fanned across her cheeks. "Talk about feeling silly—that'll sure do it. But I am so grateful you were here. For a short person like me, that was a long drop. And that you got to me so *quick*. How fast are you, anyway?"

She talked with the speed of light and Rowdy had a hard time keeping up. "Fast enough, but clearly not as fast as you talk." He chuckled.

"*Ha,* it's a curse! I do tend to rattle on when I've

been saved from sure disaster." She stood up—which wasn't all that much farther from the ground.

Rowdy wasn't real sure she was even five foot, and knew she wasn't when he stood up and looked down at her. At only six feet himself, he towered over her by a good twelve inches…which would make hugging a little awkward, but hey, he could overcome.

"I'm Lucy Calvert." She stared up at him and held out her hand.

Lucy. He liked it. Liked more the tingle of awareness that sparked the moment he took her small hand in his. When her eyes flared, as if she felt the same spark, his mind went blank.

"Rowdy. Rowdy McDermott, at your service," he said as his pulse kicked up like a stampede of wild horses.

"Rowdy." She slipped her hand free and tugged the edge of her collared shirt closed. Her smile faltered. "I think I may have heard my uncle mention you—I think he said your name fit you."

The disapproval he detected in her voice snapped him out of his infatuated fog as regret of the life he'd led twisted inside his gut. What exactly had his old neighbor said about him?

"It fits, but in all honesty, I'm trying hard to mend my ways."

"Oh." Her blue eyes dug deep. "What were you here for before I literally threw myself at you?"

"Food," he said, feeling off balance by the way she studied him. "My, um, my grandmother made you a casserole and I'm the delivery boy."

"How sweet of her." She laid her hand on his arm

and his pulse kicked again. "And of you for bringing it over."

Rowdy wasn't sure he'd ever been called sweet. He looked down at her hand on his arm as that same buzz of electricity took his breath away. She turned, hips swaying and arms pumping as she headed toward the exit and left him in her dust.

"Tell her thank you for me," she called over her shoulder, keeping her steps lively without looking back.

Rowdy followed.

"Can I ask what you were doing up there knocking out walls in your barn?"

They'd made it into the sunshine, and what had appeared to be her dark blond hair glistened like gold in the sun. She was getting better by the minute.

"I'm starting my remodel job. I'm making an art studio up there and a wall was in my way."

"So you knocked it down. Do you do that with everything that gets in your way?" That got him the smile he was looking for. Trying to put her more at ease, he tucked his fingers into the pockets of his jeans and assumed a relaxed stance, putting his weight on one leg.

"I like to hope I do."

"Really?"

Her brows leveled over suddenly serious eyes. "*Really.* That happens to be my new life motto."

"Sounds kind of drastic, don't you think?"

"Nope. Sounds good to me. It felt quite pleasant actually—" she scowled "—until I flew over the edge of the loft."

"The little woman has anger issues," he teased.

"This little woman has a *lot* of anger issues."

Rowdy knew a lot about anger issues, but would

rather not discuss them. Trying to figure out a change-of-topic comeback, he caught a movement out of the corner of his eye.

"Uh-oh," he groaned, looking where he'd left the casserole. The oversize yellow cat had ripped through the foil and was face-first in the Cowboy Goulash. "Nana isn't going to be happy about that." Even so, Rowdy was grateful for the distraction from the conversation as Lucy raced toward the cat, arms waving.

He owed the hulking orange cat big-time.

"No!" Lucy yelled, tearing across the yard with the troubling cowboy on her heels. She was not happy with her reactions to the magnetic man. Not only had he saved her, he'd taken her breath away. And she didn't like the air being sucked out of her. Nope. Not at all.

What was more, the fact that he—that any man— could do that to her was shocking.

"Bad kitty," she admonished Moose when she reached him. The cat had adopted Lucy four days ago when she'd arrived. Now the moose of a cat—thus his name—looked up at her with a goulash-orange smile, then promptly buried his head in the noodles again. "Hey, how much can a hairy beast like you eat?" Lucy asked, pulling him away from the pan as his claws dug in, clinging to the wood.

"Shame on you. Shame, shame." Lucy was so embarrassed. "Honest, I feed him. I really do."

Rowdy chuckled. "In the cat's defense, Nana's food is pretty irresistible."

Lucy's gaze met his and her insides did that crazy thing they'd been doing since the moment she'd found herself in his arms.

"I would have loved to find that out for myself," she snapped.

He gave a lazy, attractive grin. "Don't worry, Nana will be coming by soon to invite you over for dinner. She figures you need to feel welcomed, but also she wants to introduce you to our wild bunch over at Sunrise Ranch. We can be a little overwhelming for some."

His odd statement stirred her curiosity. "And how's that?"

"So you don't *know.* You're living next door to a boys' ranch."

"A boys' ranch—what do you mean exactly?" Envisioning a bunch of delinquents, Lucy felt her spirits plummet.

"No, no, I didn't mean to make you worry. They're good kids. We have a foster program of sorts. There are sixteen boys ranging from eight to eighteen who call our family ranch home. They've just had some hard knocks in their lives and we're providing a stable place for them to grow up. Speaking of which, I need to run, they're waiting on me." Grinning, he started backing away. "No more flying, okay?"

Lucy laughed despite feeling off-kilter and uneasy. "I'll keep that in mind," she said, and then he was gone. The unease didn't leave with him.

After the betrayal and nightmare she'd been through with her ex-husband, she was stunned by the buzz of attraction she'd felt toward her new neighbor.

Especially since he'd admitted being a reformed rowdy cowboy. *Reformed*—that alone was all the deterrent she needed to keep her distance. Fuzzy warm feelings or thoughts of cozying up to cute cowboys hadn't crossed her mind. Even to feel attraction at all was startling to her. Then again, the man had swooped in and saved her from breaking her neck—maybe that explained away the attraction.

The thought had Lucy breathing a little easier. She'd come here to find the joy again. Joy in her life and in her painting: things she'd lost and desperately needed to find again. She was praying that God would help her and show her the way. What she wasn't praying for was romance, relationships or attraction. She'd learned the hard way that there was no joy to be found there.

None at all. Nope, this ole girl was just fine on her own, swan diving out of the hayloft and all.

The day after he'd caught her falling out of the hayloft, Rowdy drove up Lucy's driveway again as Toby Keith played on the radio. He had a ranch to run and horses that needed training, so what was he doing back here?

Making sure she wasn't dangling from the roof. He chuckled as the thought flashed through his mind.

Stepping out of his truck, he looked up at the eaves just to make sure she wasn't doing just that.

All clear; nothing but a rooster weather vane creaking in the breeze.

Looking around, the first thing he noticed was a large pile of barn wood a few yards from the barn. It was after five and, by the looks of the pile, she'd been busy.

He had work to do, but he hadn't been able to get his new neighbor off his mind. True, he couldn't get those pretty eyes out of his head or that cute figure he sensed beneath that oversize shirt she'd been wearing, but mostly he hadn't been able to stop thinking about her over here ripping her property apart all by herself.

He shouldn't have left the day before without offering to help, and that he'd done just that had bugged him all night. He'd been taught better by his nana; buying the property for himself had vanished with Lucy showing up. And though he hated that, he didn't hold it against his new neighbor— Well, maybe a bit. But that shouldn't have stopped him from helping her.

He was headed toward the barn when Lucy came out of the back door carrying an armload of Sheetrock pieces. She wore her protective goggles again and another long-sleeved work shirt. Her jeans were tucked into a pair of low-heeled brown boots. How could a woman look that good in that get-up? He must be losing his mind.

Tucking a thumb in his waistband, he gave her a skeptical look. "So I'm thinkin' you have something against walls."

"Yup." She chuckled as she strode past him to toss the load in her arms on the pile with the other discards. "I like open space. Don't you?"

"Yeah, but you do know a house has to have some walls inside it to hold the roof up?"

She paused. "I've left a few."

"But have you left the right ones? Maybe you should hire some help. I know some contractors who could do this for you. Safely."

She stared at him for a moment, a wrinkle forming above her goggles. It suddenly hit him that she didn't look like she was in a good mood.

"Did you have a reason for stopping by?"

So he was right. "I just dropped by to check on you. Make sure you weren't dangling from high places."

The crease above her goggles deepened. "Actually, I've managed a whole day without mishap. Of course, there was a tense moment when I climbed up on the roof and lost my balance walking the peak."

His blood pressure spiked even as he recognized she was teasing him—so maybe she wasn't in a bad mood after all. "I'm glad you're teasing me."

"Had you there for a moment, though."

"Yes, you did."

She smiled sweetly. "The thing is, Rowdy, I just met you yesterday, and while I am very grateful that you saved my neck, I really don't know you. And that being the case… Well, you get what I'm saying?"

Get out of my business. Okay, so maybe she was in a bad mood—twinkling eyes and all. He was losing his touch reading women. That was an understatement. He hadn't read Liz right at all. Not until her husband had shown up and punched him in the nose had he suspected he'd gotten involved with a married woman. His stomach soured just thinking about it.

Looking at Lucy, he held his hands up. "You are absolutely right." He planned to leave it at that, get in his truck and hit the road; after all, it wasn't any of his business. The problem: Rowdy was known for not always doing what he was supposed to do. He'd suffered from the ailment all of his life.

"But you don't know what you're doing."

The words were out of his mouth before he could edit them.

Lucy's eyes flashed fire his way before she spun on

her boot heels and strode back into the house, leaving him standing just off the porch.

Clearly the woman did not want to hear what he had to say. Any man with good sense would get in his truck and head home to tend to his own business. There was sure no shortage of it and that work was what he'd promised himself and the Lord he was going to do for the next year.

But what did he do?

He followed her. That's what.

Right through her back door and in the direction of a sledgehammer beating the stuffing out of a hunk of wood somewhere inside the house.

All the while telling himself he needed to mind his own business. He had a well-thought-out plan for his life—he was done jumping off into relationships impulsively. He'd given himself at least a year to be completely single. He'd made the deal with the Lord—no attachments—and he'd almost made it.

So what are you doing?

Chapter Two

Leave it to her to get a nosy, *arrogant* cowboy for a neighbor!

What was his problem? Who was he to come here and question her intelligence? Did he really think she'd be stupid enough to knock out the walls that held her house together?

Lucy swung the sledgehammer and took unusual pleasure when it hit the two-by-four stud exactly where she'd aimed—where it connected to the wood on the bottom of the frame.

She'd been startled to walk outside and find him standing there looking all masculine and intriguing… Why did she keep thinking of him like that? Since the fire—since Tim's betrayal—she'd been around men, some even more handsome than Rowdy McDermott. But she'd not given them a second thought, other than to acknowledge that she was done with men. When a woman learned she'd been married to the poster boy for extramarital affairs, those scars weren't easy to heal.

Why, then, had she thought about her new neighbor off and on ever since he'd left the day before?

Maddeningly, he'd been the last thought she'd had going to bed and the first upon waking. Swearing off men had suited her. She swung the sledgehammer again, feeling the point of impact with a deep satisfaction. God forgive her, but she knew visualizing Tim every time she swung was not a good thing. Yet it was the best satisfaction she'd had since that woman had walked into her hospital room and exposed the lie Lucy's life had been.

Lucy swung again, harder this time. Her hands hurt with the jarring impact as the hammerhead met the solid stud.

No. She did not appreciate the cowboy showing up and causing her to realize just how much she longed to be able to trust someone. And why was it exactly that Rowdy McDermott had her thinking about trust?

She would never trust a man again.

"Well, I guess that answers my question."

Lucy jumped, so caught up in her thoughts that she hadn't heard Rowdy come into the room.

The humor in his voice was unmistakable.

"What is that supposed to mean?" she snapped. She hadn't really expected walking away from him would make him leave. So it really didn't surprise her that he'd followed her inside. After all, he had already proved he was nosy.

"You don't like walls. And you need help."

Of all the nerve. "If you must know, I planned to hire help." She yanked off her protective eyewear with one hand and set the sledgehammer against the wall— getting the thing out of her hand might be the smartest thing. "And again, *if* you must know, I was enjoying myself too much to do it."

He'd stopped smiling at her angry outburst, looking a little shocked. Now that infuriatingly cocky grin spread again across his features, like a man who knows he's charming.

Well, he wasn't to her.

"Stop that," she blurted out. His grin deepened and his eyes crinkled at the edges. He was fighting off laughter—*at her!*

"So you're angry with someone, and knocking out walls satisfies a need inside of you. I get it now. For a little thing, you really do have a lot of anger issues."

Her jaw dropped and she gasped. "Of all the—"

"How about if I help you out?"

"Do *what?*" The man had pegged her motives somewhat correctly at first guess. Yet if he only knew of the anger issues buried so far back inside her, he would not be grinning at her like that.

"Hire me—I'm cheap and will work just to watch the fireworks. You put on one entertainingly explosive show."

"This is outrageous," she huffed. Crossing her arms, she shot daggers at him—he'd think explosive. "I bet you don't get many dates, do you?"

He chuckled deep in his chest and her insides curled like a kitten in response. "We aren't talking about my love life. We're talking about me helping you out."

Lucy could not get her foot out of her mouth. She should never have mentioned anything to do with dating. Talk about getting into someone's business!

"Well," she faltered, still stuck on that chuckle.

"Look, like I said yesterday," Rowdy continued, "my nana is going to have you over to dinner next week and if she finds out you need help and I didn't do the neighborly thing and help you, believe me, it won't be pretty. So help a fella out and put me to work."

Despite everything, Lucy found herself wanting to smile. But the past reared its ugly face—this was so like Tim.

How many times had he cajoled her into doing something he wanted? *Too many.* The fist of mistrust knotted beneath her ribs.

"I'll think about it," she said, having meant to tell him no. She repositioned her goggles.

He frowned. "Fine. I'll let you get back to your work, then."

Irritation had his shoulders stiff as she watched him leave. She almost called out to him, but didn't. She'd given in to Tim too many times in her life. Why did men believe women were supposed to just stop thinking for themselves whenever they were in the picture?

Lucy wasn't going down that road again. The screen door slammed in the other room, and a few seconds later she heard his truck's engine rumble to life. Drawn to the window, she watched him back out onto the hardtop. But he didn't leave immediately. Instead, he sat with his arm hooked over the steering wheel, staring at the house. Though he couldn't see her, she felt as if he were looking straight at her.

She stepped back and he drove off. Her heart thumped erratically as she watched him disappear in the distance.

It's better this way.

It certainly was.

Then why did she suddenly feel so lonely she could scream?

* * *

"Women," Rowdy growled, driving away. "They drive me crazy." She could just knock her whole house down for all he cared. He had things to do and places to be and being the Good Samaritan was obviously not his calling. It was his own fault—he should have minded his stinkin' business.

After only a short drive down the blacktop road, he turned onto the ranch, spinning gravel as he drove beneath the thick log entrance with the Sunrise Ranch logo overhead.

Dust flying behind him, he sped toward the ranch house in the distance, its roof peeking up over the hill that hid the majority of the ranch compound from the road.

The compound of Sunset Ranch had been divided into sections. The first section was the main house, the ranch office and the Chow Hall, where his grandmother, Ruby Ann "Nana" McDermott, ruled the roost. For sixteen boys ranging in age from eight to eighteen the Chow Hall was the heart of the ranch. But Nana was actually the heart.

Across the gravel parking area, the hundred-year-old horse stable stretched out. Most every horse he'd ever trained had been born in the red, wooden building since the day his grandfather had bought the place years ago. Beside the horse stable stood the silver metal barn and the large corral and riding pens. Making up the last section was the three-room private school the ranch provided for the kids. It sat out from the rest of the compound, within easy walking distance, to give the kids space from school life. This was home.

Rowdy pulled the truck to a stop beside the barn.

He slammed the door with the rest of the disgust he was feeling just as his brother Morgan walked out of the barn.

"What bee's in your bonnet?" Morgan asked.

Rowdy scowled. "Funny."

"Obviously something is wrong."

All the McDermott brothers were dark headed, square chinned and sported the McDermott navy eyes, but Morgan was the brother who most resembled their dad—steadfast. Respectable.

Rowdy had always lived up to his more reckless looks—good-time Rowdy. That had been him. But he'd turned a corner and was trying hard to be more than a "good time." And that misconception irritated him the most about Lucy turning down his offer to help. It was almost as if she saw his past and chose to bypass trouble. As if she'd decided in that moment she couldn't trust him.

The thought pricked. Stung like a wasp, to be honest.

If she couldn't trust the man who caught her swan diving off the hayloft, then who could she trust?

And why did he care?

Morgan crossed his arms and studied him. "Nana tells me you met our new neighbor yesterday. Does this have something to do with her?"

"No. Maybe. Yeah."

"So what did you do?"

"I saved her from breaking her neck falling out of her hayloft, Morg. And I offered to help her do a little remodeling."

"I see. So that'd mean she must be good-looking."

"Yeah, she is," he growled.

"Then why are you so agitated? She's single, from what Nana said."

"She turned me down."

Morgan blinked in disbelief. "Turned *you* down. You?"

It was embarrassing in more ways than one.

"I don't think that's ever happened before." Morgan started grinning. "And did you actually save her from falling out of the hayloft?"

"Stop enjoying this so much, and yes, I did, and it's not like I asked her out." He knew Morgan was just giving him a hard time. That was what brothers did. He'd never missed an opportunity where Morgan and Tucker were concerned. So much so that he was due a lot of payback from both brothers. He gave a quick rundown of catching Lucy the day before. Morgan's grin spread as wide as Texas.

"So you really didn't ask her out?"

"Are you kidding? No."

Morgan cocked his head to the side, leveling disbelieving eyes on him. "Are you feeling okay?"

"Crazy, isn't it? I'm not saying I'm not going to. But my days of rushing into relationships are done. I told you that."

"Yeah you did, but it's been over nine months."

Rowdy wanted on a horse. Needed to expel the restless energy that suddenly filled him. "I wasn't kidding when I said I was done with women for at least a year. I'm trying to be a role model for the guys."

It was true. Rowdy might not have known he'd gotten involved with a married woman, but then he hadn't really asked enough questions, and he sure hadn't been any kind of role model. After this last fiasco, God had convinced him that he needed to change his life.

"You're doing it, too. What you need is to find a woman like Jolie, who has her priorities straight," Morgan added.

"True, but I'm not ready right now. And besides, if Lucy won't let me help knock out some walls, she's most definitely not going to say yes to dinner and a movie."

"True," Morgan agreed, clapping him on the shoulder. "Speaking of dates, Tucker's here helping out with practice because I've got a date. And Jolie is a whole lot prettier than you."

"Tell that beautiful lady of yours I said hello," he called, then headed into the stable. He breathed in and the scents of fresh hay and leather filled him. Horses nickered as he passed by.

He grabbed a saddle and entered the stall of the black quarter horse he was working with. He spoke gently to Maverick as he saddled him. Just the motions of preparing to ride calmed him and helped him think.

Lucy said she had anger issues. It didn't fit, but she'd said it. He hadn't seen anger, though. When their eyes locked, he saw fireworks. And there lay the problem.

He had a fondness for fireworks—even though the fondness had gotten him into more trouble than he needed. Thus the reason he was trying to mend his ways.

Fireworks burned—he'd learned that the hard way.

Leading Maverick out of the stable, he headed toward the corral and the sound of whoops of laughter. His behavior hadn't been anything to be proud of and certainly nothing for these boys to look up to. Rowdy was changing that. No one had said it would be easy.

And living his lifestyle down was going to be the hardest of all, he suspected. The boys' laughter rose on the breeze out in the arena as he approached. This was what he needed to concentrate on. These boys and the ranch.

"What's up, Rowdy? Thought you'd skipped out on us." Eighteen years old, Wes gave him his wolfish smile as he rode his horse over to the arena fence.

"Nope, just running late." Rowdy hooked his arms on the top rail and surveyed the action. "Did I miss much?"

"There was a runaway wagon a few minutes ago when Caleb lost his grip on the reins and the horses took over." Wes chuckled, his blue eyes sparkling with mischief. He was one of the natural leaders of the group. Stocky and blond, he always looked as though he was ready to have a good time. Too good. He had a recklessness about him that reminded Rowdy of himself. All the more reason for Rowdy to make a good impression on the teen.

Rowdy had a suspicion Wes had been sneaking around riding bulls behind everyone's back. Bulls were the one rodeo event that was off-limits for the ranch kids to participate in. And purely Rowdy's fault from when he'd been a teen. Because of his many close calls with bull riding, his dad had set the rule—no bull riding at Sunrise Ranch.

"By the glint in your eyes, I'm assuming it was pretty entertaining."

"It was awesome." Wes hooted. "I never knew your

brother could ride like that. Tucker did some pony tricks getting the horses to stop."

The sheriff of Dew Drop, Tucker didn't spend as much time on the ranch with the boys as Rowdy, Morgan and their dad, Randolph. But when it came to riding, Tucker could hold his own.

"I'm glad Caleb was okay." He glanced out into the arena and saw Tucker talking to a group of the younger kids.

"He's fine. Didn't even shake him up." Wes spit a sunflower seed in the dirt and continued grinning.

Rowdy suddenly had an idea. It might not be a good idea, but that was yet to be seen. "Wes, I need you and Joseph to help me with something in the morning. Can you do it?"

"Sure thing. What are we going to do?"

More than likely make Lucy madder than a hornet. "We're going to do a little yard work and y'all can make a little pocket change."

"*Sweet.* When do we start?"

"Sunup."

"Sounds like a plan to me." A group of the boys over by the chutes called for Wes. "Showtime. I'll tell Joseph." Giving his horse a nudge, they raced off at a thundering gallop.

Rowdy watched him and the horse fly across the arena as one. When it came to riding, Wes was the best. He was a natural. Rowdy had a feeling the kid would ride a bull just as well. Though it was against the rules, Rowdy hesitated to say anything until he knew for certain. Wes was courting trouble...but then so was Rowdy if he went through with his plan in the morning.

What was he thinking, anyway?

The woman didn't want his help. She needed it, though, and for reasons he didn't quite understand he felt compelled to follow through—despite knowing he needed to steer clear of her.

He had a feeling he was about to see some major fireworks tomorrow…but he'd rather take that chance than do nothing at all.

Chapter Three

The morning light was just crawling across her bed-room floor when Lucy opened her eyes. She'd been dead to the world from the moment she'd fallen into bed late last night, and she stared at the ceiling for a moment, disoriented.

The ache in her arms brought clarity quickly.

And no wonder with all the manual labor she'd been doing for the past week. The muscle soreness had finally caught up with her last night. Caught up with her back, too. She'd always had a weak lower back and sometimes after a lot of stooping and heavy lifting, it rebelled on her. That moment had happened when she'd taken her last swing at the long wall in her living room—a muscle spasm had struck her like a sledgehammer.

It had been so painful she'd been forced to stretch out on the floor and stare at the ceiling until it had eased up enough for her to make it upstairs to bed.

She'd had plenty of time to contemplate her situation and the fact that she really had no timeline to finish her remodel. She could take all the time in the world if she wanted to. Uncle Harvey, bless his soul, had made sure of that.

He was actually her grandfather's brother, whom she'd lost as a young girl. He had been in bad health when her world had fallen apart, and hadn't lived on the ranch for a couple of years. But he'd told her this was where she needed be. And he'd been right. She'd known it the moment she'd arrived. She was making the place her own and searching for her new footing at the same time.

And yet, things had changed when Rowdy McDermott had offered to help her. She watched him drive off, and her conscience had plucked away at her.

To prove that she'd made the right decision turning him away, she'd gone at her work with extra zeal…but the pleasure she'd felt had disappeared. Drat the man—he'd messed up her process.

He'd had no right trying to take over her work. *He was only being a good neighbor.* The voice of reason she'd been steadily ignoring yesterday was louder this morning. Had she judged him wrong? She didn't like this distrust that ruled her life these days.

Sitting up, she had no control of the groan that escaped her grimacing lips. "Hot shower, really hot shower." She eased off the bed and walked stiffly toward the bathroom.

She'd wash the cobwebs out of her mind, the dust out of her hair and the pain out of her muscles. Then maybe she could figure out what she needed to do about the problems her good-looking neighbor was causing her.

She'd told him she would think about his offer. But did she really want him here? And he'd already shown that he thought his way was the best way. Did she want to fight that? Because she wasn't giving up control of anything.

The niggling admission that she might be in over her head and needed help on this simmered in her thoughts. The realization that she was allowing distrust of men— all men—color her need for real help bothered her.

Shower, now! She needed a clear head to sort this out.

Twenty minutes later, feeling better, she padded down to the kitchen. The shower had helped her spirits, but she knew that today her back was going to give her fits if she did anything too strenuous. It needed a break. Her mind needed a break, too. She couldn't shut it off....

When a gal wasn't quite five feet tall, she grew used to people assuming she was helpless because of her size. Too weak to swing a sledgehammer.

It was maddening. More so now—since her husband's betrayal had left her feeling so pathetically blind and weak-minded.

Too weak to realize my husband was cheating on me.

The humiliating thought slipped into her head like the goad of an enemy. Not the best way to start her day. She was going to miss not knocking out a wall—and the satisfaction it gave her.

People's lack of faith always made her all the more determined to do whatever it was they assumed she couldn't do.

Glancing down at her wrists, she could see the puckered skin peeking out from the edge of her long-sleeved T-shirt. She knew those scars looked twisted and savage as they covered her arm and much of her body beneath her clothing. The puckered burn scars on her neck itched, reminding her how close she'd come to having her face disfigured…reminding her of her blessings amid the tragedy that had become her life two years ago.

She hadn't felt blessed then, when she'd nearly died in the fire that had killed her husband.

And learned the truth she hadn't seen before.

Reaching for the coffeepot, her fingers trembled. There had been days during the year she'd spent in the burn center that she'd wished she hadn't survived. But it was the internal scars from Tim's betrayal that were the worst.

Those scars weren't as easy to heal. But they made knocking walls out a piece of cake. She'd just overdone it. Easy to do when there was enough anger inside her 105-pound frame to knock walls down for years.

Each swing made her feel stronger. She might have lost control of her life two years ago, but thanks to her dear uncle thinking about her in his will, she was here in Dew Drop, Texas, determined to regain control.

On her terms.

And knocking out walls was just the beginning. Just as Uncle Harvey had intended. He'd recognized that she was struggling emotionally and floundering to find meaning in it all after finally being released from the hospital.

Walking to the sink, she flipped on the cold water and looked out the window as she stuck the pot under the spray. Two young men were carrying fallen tree branches to her burn pile!

Lucy jumped at the unexpected sight and sloshed water on herself. Setting the pot down, she grabbed a dishrag and wiped her hands as she headed for the door. *What is going on?*

She stormed out onto her back porch and caught her breath when Rowdy stepped around the corner.

"You," she gasped. "I should have known. What is going on here?" This was what she was talking about—control. "Just because you saved me doesn't give you the right to just disregard my wishes—"

"Look, I knew you needed help. I just brought the fellas over to pick up a few limbs for you."

Teens, not men, watching them from the burn pile, clearly uncertain whether to come near or not. They could probably see steam shooting out of her ears.

"They've cleaned up a lot. We've been at it since about six."

"Six!" It was eight-thirty now. How had she not heard them?

"We tried to be quiet so we wouldn't wake you."

Her mouth fell open. What did he think he was doing?

"You were quiet because you didn't want me to know you were here."

His eyes flashed briefly. "I wanted to surprise you."

"You just can't take no for an answer."

He stared at her, his jaw tensed, and a sense of guilt overcame her. Guilt. He was the one who should be guilty.

Right?

She was glaring at him when his gaze drifted to her neck and it was only then that she realized she hadn't pulled on her work shirt yet over her long-sleeved T-shirt.

He was staring at the scar. It licked up from the

back of her neck, out from the protection of her hair, and curled around, stopping jaggedly just below her jawline.

"You've been burned." There was shock in his voice.

"Yes." Turning, she went back into the house to get the work shirt draped over the kitchen chair. Her hands shook as she slipped it on. Rowdy barreled inside behind her.

"Lucy, I'm sorry we startled you like we did. You have every right to be angry."

Angry? She could barely think, she was so embarrassed. Striding to the living room, she grabbed for her sledgehammer, and without putting on her goggles she took a swing at the wall. Her back and shoulders lashed out at her, forcing her to set the hammer down immediately. She was being ridiculous and she knew it. Why was she so afraid to let Rowdy help her?

The man was obstinate, that was why. Arrogant even, by showing up here to work anyway.

"I'm sorry about that burn. It looks like it must have been terribly painful."

She met his gaze and gave him a quick nod. Her scars were something she didn't talk about. Especially the ones on the inside. "It's fine now," she said bluntly. She hoped he'd take the hint and not continue this line of talk.

"Look—" he shifted from boot to boot and scrubbed the back of his neck in a show of frustration "—you need help and you know it. You said yesterday that you would think about it. I was just trying to let you see that the guys were good kids and hard workers. They could whip this yard into shape for you in no time.

And they'll do it for free. C'mon, give them a chance. Give *me* a chance."

As aggravating as it was to admit—the man had charm. And there was no way to deny that she needed help. She couldn't go through life shunning all men. That was unrealistic. The fact he'd seen a portion of her scars ate into her confidence, and that was maddening. It did not matter what the cowboy thought of her.

It didn't.

"Why not?" she heard herself saying. "It looks like you're going to be over here every day bothering me anyway. But just for a few days. And I'll pay you." *Lucy! What are you doing?*

A slow smile spread across his face. "There you go. That wasn't so hard after all, was it?" he said, reaching for her sledgehammer. "No pay needed for me, but if you want to pay the boys, that's fine. I was going to pay them for today myself."

"I'll pay them for today."

"No, I said I would—"

"Look, Rowdy," Lucy said, in her sternest voice. "If they are going to be over here, then I'm paying them. It's either that or this deal is off." They stared at each other and she got the distinct impression that he didn't "get" her in the same way that she didn't get him. But she was taking back control of this situation, or she wasn't having any part of it.

"Okay, have it your way."

"Good."

"All righty, then, stand back," he warned.

Lucy felt her body automatically obey, and watched him swing the heavy sledgehammer as if it was a plastic toy. The muscles in his forearms strained with the strength he put behind the swing. The hammer met the same spot her swing had barely dented and instantly the wood cracked beneath it.

She brought her hand up and touched the base of her throat where her heartbeat raced.

After three more swings along the base of the studded wall, it broke free. It would have taken her all day to do that!

"I see what attracts you to this." He looked over his shoulder at her with a teasing light in his eyes. "I kinda like it myself."

"Yeah, it does kill a bad mood, doesn't it?"

He laughed at that and they stared at each other. Tension radiated between them.

"Okay," she said at last. "Thank you for helping me. I did need it."

"No need to thank me." His smile widened. "You're the one helping me. Saving me from the wrath of Nana is a good thing. If there is one thing she prides above all else, it's that her boys are gentlemen. And I have to admit I have sometimes been her wayward child."

"Say it ain't so," Lucy mocked.

"Yeah, but I'm gonna make points when she finds out about this. So I guess that means I'm still the wayward child, since I'm really doing this for myself. Does that make you feel any better about letting me swing away?"

"Much better. I'd hate for you to actually admit that you're doing it because you're a nice guy." And he might be, even if he was a little nosy. But that didn't stop her from being wary...not so much of him, but of the way she reacted to him.

"Me, a nice guy." He looked skeptical, and that grin played across his face. "I don't know about that."

The man's personality sparkled and drew her like his eyes and his smile, stunning her once again.

Had she truly thought she was going to go the rest of her life not finding a man attractive?

Of course not.

That her neighbor just happened to have qualities that, regrettably, reminded her that she was still a woman, meant nothing. Absolutely nothing.

She was still telling herself that when Ruby Ann McDermott, Rowdy's grandmother, showed up at her house midmorning bearing welcome-to-Dew-Drop gifts: a basket loaded with homemade fig and strawberry preserves and green tomato relish, along with several small loaves of banana-nut bread to freeze and take out as needed, she informed Lucy.

Ruby Ann had long silver hair pulled back in a ponytail and strong features like Rowdy, along with those deep blue eyes the color of a twilight sky. She held her tall frame ramrod straight, with an elegance about the way she moved.

Two friends came along with her. The first of them, Ms. Jo, owned the Spotted Cow Café in town. Lucy had met her the day she'd first arrived. She'd had supper at the cute café after spending the day unpacking. Ms. Jo's piercing hazel eyes seemed to take everything in from behind her wire-rimmed glasses. She wore her slate-gray hair in a soft cap of curls. Lucy felt a kindred spirit, not just from the fact that they were close to the same height. She liked the older lady's spunk and hoped her own personality would be similar when she was nearing seventy.

Ms. Jo brought along a coconut pie that looked so mouthwateringly delicious Lucy could barely keep from diving in the instant Ms. Jo placed it in her hands.

Mabel Tilsbee, the other member of the welcoming committee, owned the Dew Drop Inn. The towering, large-boned woman with shoulder-length black hair spiced with just a few strands of gray handed over a tray of cookies that were clearly overdone. "There's no need in me even pretending to be the best in the kitchen when the county's best are both standing here beside me. I gave it a whirl, though." She winked. "I got distracted and baked these a little too long. But, if you like coffee, they're real good dunkers."

Lucy laughed and felt instantly at home with these ladies. "Thank you all so much for coming by," she said, leading them into the kitchen. They eyed where a wall had obviously just been knocked out.

Ruby Ann's hand fluttered at the construction area. "Rowdy told me at breakfast this morning that he helped you do this. And that he and some of the boys will be helping you out for a little while."

"Yes, ma'am, he did." It was all Lucy could do not to smile at the thought of Rowdy's brownie points. She decided to help him out. "He's doing a great job. I worked almost two days knocking a wall out of the hayloft and half the morning just getting this wall to budge. He had it down within an hour. It was quite humiliating."

That got a chuckle from everyone.

"All my boys are strong and know how to work," Ruby Ann said.

"That's the truth." Ms. Jo's eyes sparkled with mischief. "Handsome, too, wouldn't you say?"

"Yes, he is." She couldn't deny the obvious. "I was just about to have a coffee break when y'all drove up. Please join me. I suddenly have lots of great food to choose from."

"You know, hon—" Mabel gave her a nudge with her elbow "—that's a *great* idea. I'll slice the pie."

Lucy headed for the cups. This move was getting better by the day.

Mabel took the knife she handed her and sliced the pie and one of the loaves of banana-nut bread, instantly filling Lucy's kitchen with mouthwatering aromas.

She filled four mugs with coffee and in a matter of minutes they were all gathered around her kitchen table laughing and talking between bites.

An hour later, with an official invitation to dinner the next evening, she waved goodbye and was smiling as she watched her new friends drive away.

Her mother called this Nowhere, U.S.A., but to Lucy, this small town felt like home.

Turning back, she surveyed the low-slung ranch house. Three days ago, overgrown shrubs had threatened to obscure it, and one of the shutters had needed to be straightened. Not so since Wes, Joseph and Rowdy had stepped in.

Ever since she'd awakened in the hospital to discover the truth about her life, she'd been adrift and searching for something. Only her faith that God was beside her had gotten her through. And her God-given stubbornness.

From his perch on the porch railing, Moose purred,

and even that from the ornery tomcat felt like a welcome—after all, he'd picked her.

"Yes, big fellow," Lucy murmured, lifting him up and hugging him, "I do believe us two strays have found our home."

Rowdy McDermott's image plopped right back into her contented thoughts, settling in like a sticker poking through a sock.

Pushing the irritating worry aside, she headed inside to reread her home-repair guide on plastering a wall. She might have trust issues by the wagonload, but she was not a chicken.

She would not allow her fears to send her running.

She'd taken her first step toward starting over, and this was where she was making her stand.

Dew Drop was where Lucy Calvert took control of her life again.

Chapter Four

"Excuse me, ma'am. But you want me to do what?"

Rowdy's lips twitched as he watched tall, lanky Joseph staring down at Lucy with a look of complete confusion. Always ready to please, the kid usually wore an affable grin, but right now he looked almost in shock. On Saturday Lucy had talked to them in-depth about what she wanted the yard to look like and they'd done a fantastic job. But they hadn't been inside the house.

For example, they didn't know until now that Lucy had a thing about walls. That the only good wall to her was a torn-out wall. He tugged on his ear and watched the show, enjoying every minute of it.

"I want you to take this sledgehammer," Lucy said, "and I want you to take a whack at this wall. It's fun! Believe me. It's freedom in a swing."

"Oh, I believe you," Joseph said. "It's just you already knocked out that wall over there, and I wasn't sure I was hearing you right. I mean, this one's a perfectly good wall and all."

Wes was champing at the bit to swing the sledgehammer. "Knock that dude down, bro. Or I'll do it."

Lucy chuckled. "I want this house opened up. It's too closed in. I like big airy rooms with lots of light. And, fellas, I've got to tell you that your Texas manners are perfect. Y'all have about ma'amed me to death. But you can call me Lucy from here on out. Got it?"

"Yes, ma'am—I mean, Lucy," Joseph complied, taking the sledgehammer and grinning as he looked from it to the blue wall. "I guess I can give this a go."

"Oh, yeah." Wes rubbed his palms together gleefully. "Swing away, Joe."

Rowdy's shoulders shook in silent laughter as Joseph pulled his protective eyewear down, then reared back and swung. A large hole busted through one side of the Sheetrock into the next room. It didn't take any more encouragement after that. The two teens started taking turns whacking away at the long wall that separated the living room from the den. The wall Rowdy had knocked out had been the divider for the kitchen and living room. What had once been three small dark rooms was now going to be one large space. He had to admit it was going to look good when it was all over with.

If she didn't knock *all* the walls out. The thought had him smiling and he almost said something to set her off, even though he knew she was leaving the load-bearing wall.

"Those have got to be the sweetest boys," she said, walking over to him. "Thank you for suggesting they come help me out. I think Joseph thought I had a few screws loose or something."

"He's on board now, though." Rowdy was curious about Lucy. She was an artist, though he'd yet to see any sign of art anywhere. He suddenly wondered about that. Her house was still loaded down with boxes and the walls were bare. Probably a good thing while she was stirring up all this dust. But was there more to it? His brothers had always called him the curious one. And his curiosity was working double time on Lucy.

As if sensing he was watching her, she turned her head and met his gaze with eyes that held a hint of wariness. She looked at him often like that and it added to his curiosity. Why?

She lifted her hand to her collar and tugged it close. He'd noticed she'd done this several times before, as if self-conscious about the burn scar on her neck.

He'd wondered about the scar and what had caused it. It was obvious that whatever had happened had been painful.

Being self-conscious about anything was at odds with his image of Lucy.

"Your grandmother came by this morning with her friends. They're a great group." She waved toward the counter loaded with pie and cookies. "I have all kinds of goodies in there left over if you and the guys want to take a break."

That made him laugh. In the background the pounding grew steadily, and then something crashed and the boys' whoops rang joyfully through the house. "As you can hear, I'm not doing anything, so if you mean there's pie in there from Ms. Jo, then I'm all in."

She'd started smiling when the boys started whooping. She was one gorgeous woman.

"There's pie. And, by the way, I put in a good word for you."

She headed into the kitchen and he followed. She wore another of those oversize shirts, hot pink today, and he began to think it was an artist quirk or something. The collar brushed her jaw and the sleeves covered half her hands, they were so long. And still, as dwarfed as she was in all that cloth, he remembered the feel of her in his arms that first day.

She might be small, but Lucy Calvert was all woman.

She turned suddenly and he almost ran over her. Automatically, he wrapped his arms around her, lifting her instead of mowing her down.

"Sorry about that." He set her on her feet and she immediately put distance between them.

She gave a shaky laugh. "I'm so short it's easy to miss me."

"Hardly. No one would miss you." His frank assessment of her appeal had her swinging away from him to reach for a pie. She lifted the cover, her shoulders stiff as she did so, and he realized she didn't like him flirting with her. "I just wasn't watching where I was going," he added, trying to ease the tension that had sprung between them.

She'd started slicing pie with a vengeance. "Will you ask the boys what they'd like to drink with their pie, please?" she asked, as if he hadn't spoken.

He stared at her back for a few minutes, confused by her reaction. "Sure," he said, and went to get the guys.

What had just happened?

Lucy arrived at Sunrise Ranch with the pit of her stomach churning. She knew a lot about the ranch now, since working with Wes and Joseph. The teens had been fun to be around and had worked really hard. She'd been glad she hired them and got to watch their excitement over being destructive. And they'd been so polite doing it.

Even now the thought made her smile.

If it hadn't been for their constant exuberance, she didn't know what she'd have done when she'd found herself in Rowdy's arms once more—one minute she'd been fine and the next his muscled arms had swept her off her feet and his heartbeat was tangoing with her own.

She'd overreacted. Panicked. She'd forgotten how wonderful it felt to be held by a man.

Forgotten the feel of another heart beating against hers.

What she *hadn't* forgotten was how complete betrayal felt and that had driven her, shaken and babbling, out of his arms and across the room.

He probably thought she was crazy. Well, that made two of them.

Letting the excitement of meeting her neighbors take over, she parked beside the house like Ruby Ann had instructed her to do.

Kids were everywhere. There were several across the way in the arena riding horses, including Joseph and Wes. Three younger boys were taking turns trying to throw their ropes around the horns on a roping dummy in front of the barn. They stopped to watch as she got out of her truck and immediately, ropes dragging, they headed her way.

"You must be Lucy," the smallest boy said, arms pumping from side to side as he raced to beat his buddies. His plump cheeks were pink and dampness suffused his face. Obviously he'd been outside for a while and his oversize wide-rimmed cowboy hat hadn't completely shaded him from the sunlight.

"Yes, I am. How did you guess?"

"I heard Rowdy say you were kinda short. And you ain't much taller than me."

Ha! "True. I can't deny that you are almost as tall as me."

"I'm B.J., by the way. I'm the youngest one here, so I'm supposed to be short."

The other two crowded close. Almost the same size, one had brown hair and brown eyes, and the other was blond haired with blue eyes. They looked around nine years old and were almost her height.

"I'm Sammy and this here is Caleb," the brown-haired one said. "We heard you let Wes and Joseph knock down walls in your house. We been thinking it would be mighty fun to do. We're pretty strong. Show her your muscles, Caleb."

Immediately all arms cocked to show small bumps that would one day be muscles and truly did have some definition to them despite their young ages.

Vitality radiated from the three of them in their oversize hats, jeans, boots and B.J. with his leather vest. They could easily go on the cover of a greeting card.

"So how's the roping going?"

"Good, you wanna come try?" B.J. asked, taking her hand in his damp, slightly sticky one. "It's real fun. I ain't got it all figured out, but Caleb here, he's pretty good."

"I am, too," Sammy said, looking put out that B.J. hadn't said so. "I might be the newest kid here, but I been working real hard and almost got Caleb caught."

Lucy laughed at the competitiveness as she allowed B.J. to pull her across the gravel to the metal roping dummy. "I'll try it. But I'm not promising much."

Wes and Joseph rode up to the fence with a slightly younger kid with coal-black hair, blue eyes and a crooked grin. The skinny teen looked amazingly like a younger version of Elvis Presley, whose old movies she'd loved as a kid, watching with her mother. It was one good memory she had of time spent with her mother.

"You made it," Wes called over the rail.

"Your house didn't cave in yet, did it?" Joseph's soft-spoken teasing made her smile. He had been so skeptical about taking a swing at the wall, but in the end he'd been a wall-knocking maniac just like Wes. It was easy to see Wes lived on the edge—much like she'd picture Rowdy at that age. But Joseph, he was a gentle soul.

"No, it's still standing. At least when I left."

"We want to help, too, please," Sammy said, reiterating what B.J. had said earlier. "Wes was telling us about how you just told them to beat that wall to smithereens and we all want to take a whack at it."

Everyone started talking at once, and Lucy found herself in the midst of a huge discussion on why the younger boys should get the chance to come knock out her walls.

"Whoa, guys." She called a time-out with her hands. "I have no problem with more help. We'll set it up with Rowdy. How does that sound?"

It wasn't long before Rowdy rode up on a horse with a couple of other men—one was an older cowboy with snow-white hair introduced as Pepper, the horse fore-

man, and the other was Chet, the Sunrise Ranch top
hand. She'd learned from Nana's visit that Rowdy was
the cattle-operation manager and quarter horse trainer.
It was easy to see that Rowdy was a hands-on kind of
cowboy, dusty from whatever he'd been doing out there
on his horse. Lucy's fingers itched with the desire to
paint him and his friends as they'd looked riding in
from the open range.

She'd been struck by the Old West look of Rowdy
in his chaps and spurs. And those deep blue, dangerous eyes as they glinted in the sunlight.

Chet and Pepper led their horses into the barn and
he dismounted.

"I see the boys are making you feel at home."

"Very. They're a great bunch."

They all began talking at once and she loved it.
Their excitement was contagious.

"What are y'all practicing for?" she asked them.

"The ranch rodeo. We got to get good so we can
help our teams," B.J. said, holding his coiled rope in
the air like a trophy.

As she was not sure what the difference was between a ranch rodeo and a regular rodeo, the kids explained that at a ranch rodeo there were events done
with teams. The younger ones began telling her about
their roping skills and asking if she'd ever mugged, or
roped, a calf. Their questions were coming faster than
paintballs from a paintball gun and she was barely
keeping up.

Rowdy had crossed his arms, grinning at her as he
rocked back on his boots, enjoying her induction into
his world.

"Lucy," Ruby Ann called from the back porch of

the house across the parking lot. When Lucy turned her way, she waved. "Could you come here and give me a hand?"

"Sure, I'll be right there." She smiled at the boys and realized a couple of extras had appeared from somewhere, maybe from inside the barn. There were boys of all heights and sizes everywhere. It was going to be a test of her memory skills just to get them all connected with their names. "If you'll all excuse me, I'll see you soon."

"We've got to wash up and put horses away, and then we'll be joining you," Rowdy explained. "Nana gave the house parents a date-night pass, so you get to hang with all sixteen boys and the rest of the family tonight."

Lucy did not miss that he was including the boys in the "family." It touched her deeply. As much as she was struggling with certain aspects of being around him, this was one more glaring declaration of his being a nice guy.

Ruby Ann held the door open for her and smiled as she entered. "It's so good to have you here. Met the crew, I see." She enveloped Lucy in a welcoming hug, then led the way down the hall past the mudroom and into the expansive kitchen.

"Did I ever! I'm in love."

"I know, they'll just twist your heart and hook you in an instant, won't they?"

"They're amazing."

The scrumptious scent of baked bread and pot roast filled the house, if her nose was correct. The tantalizing scents had her stomach growling. These scents were similar to those of her grandmother's home back when she'd been alive.

"Dinner smells amazing, Ruby Ann."

"Thank you. Now take a seat, and, for goodness' sake, call me Nana. You're going to hear it chanted all through the evening by my boys."

"Nana it is." It felt comfortable and right to call her Nana. She loved that Nana called them her boys. "Is there something I can help you with?"

"I love a woman who pitches in. You can peel these grapes for the fruit salad, if you don't mind."

"Peel the grapes? Sure," she said, shocked at the request. She'd never even thought about someone peeling grapes, much less doing it herself.

Nana chuckled. "I'm just teasing. I've already peeled the grapes. But you can slice up these strawberries for me if you don't mind."

Relieved that Nana had been teasing, she sat down and took the knife Nana held out to her.

There was food everywhere. "This is amazing. How did you ever learn to cook for a group this large?"

Waving the spoon she'd been stirring cheese into a mountain of mashed potatoes with, she chuckled. "I talked to a caterer and she gave me some formulas. Now it just comes naturally. Kind of like I expect painting comes to you. Right?"

Lucy remembered the first time she'd walked into a local art studio and picked up a paintbrush. She'd been ten, and her mother had wanted to encourage her drawing ability. Lucy had loved the scents that filled the studio, linseed oil and turpentine, and the instant she'd held that brush, everything in the world had seemed suddenly right.

It had been a long time since she'd had that feeling. She smiled. "Yes, you're right. My painting is from instinct, though I had some formal training when I was young."

"I read about you, you know. Looked you up on the Net." Nana's wise eyes settled on her as she spoke.

Lucy knew if that were the case, then she knew about the fire. "You did?" she asked, trying to keep her voice steady.

Nana studied her. "You had a hard time of it. I'm sorry. How are you doing now?"

"I'm okay," she said, trying to figure out where to direct the conversation. It wasn't as if she hadn't thought that someone could check her out online. After all, she was an artist with a bit of success. A rush of sound broke into their conversation as the back door opened and one after the other of the boys streamed down the hall and through the kitchen. She wasn't sure how all of them would fit in the house.

As if reading her mind, Nana said, "We usually eat in the Chow Hall, but tonight is special, we're having a guest. So it may be a tight squeeze."

Laughter and banter filled the room as Rowdy ushered the boys into the den. His brother Morgan and his wife, Jolie, arrived and Rowdy introduced them. Not that she'd needed the introduction—their resemblance was too similar. Morgan, like Rowdy, had Nana's direct navy eyes.

"Morgan and my dad run the business side of the foster program and the ranch. Jolie has been our schoolteacher since the beginning of the year."

"I can't wait to see some of your work." Jolie's wide smile reminded Lucy instantly of Julia Roberts, especially with her auburn hair and her expressive eyes. "I envy an artist their abilities. I'm a klutz with a brush in my hand."

"I won't believe that until I see it." Lucy had the distinct impression that this lady could do anything she set her mind to. And quickly she learned it was true when Morgan told her Jolie was a champion kayaker. It was easy to see his pride in her accomplishments. Tim had always seemed threatened by her success. His greatest wish had been for her to give up her work.

Lucy was so thankful that she hadn't done that.

Looking at Morgan and Jolie, she had to admit that she envied the bond between them. Their mutual respect spoke volumes.

They all talked about her work some—that it was in galleries and that she also sold prints. She wasn't Thomas Kinkaid or Norman Rockwell, but she was blessed to have some recognition, giving her the ability to paint full-time.

It wasn't long before they were all helping carry the large platters of food to the huge table in the dining area. There were so many of them that card tables had been set up to help accommodate them all.

While they were setting the table, Rowdy's brother Tucker showed up. Introductions were made and she knew before they told her that he had been in the Special Forces. There was just something about the way he carried himself. He still wore a very close-cropped haircut she could see when he removed his Stetson and hung it on the hat rack. Rowdy's hair was more touchable, run-your-fingers-through-it type. Where both Morgan and Tucker had serious edges to their expressions, Rowdy's was more open, and—she searched for the right word—*light* was all that came to mind.

Rowdy's eyes twinkled as he wrestled on the couch with B.J. and Sammy. His infectious laughter had Lucy wanting to join in.

She brought her thoughts up short, realizing that she was comparing Rowdy's attributes with his brothers'. She had no reason to do that.

No reason and no want to.

Frustrated by her thoughts, Lucy marched back to the kitchen in search of a plate of food to carry. She needed something constructive to do. What was wrong with her, anyway?

Chapter Five

Dinner was a loud affair. But with that many boys crammed beneath one roof, it was to be expected. Rowdy enjoyed watching Lucy's reactions to the wild bunch. She handled herself pretty well for a new-comer. Then again, how he was handling himself *was* the question, as he found himself sitting next to her.

He could tell Nana had her eagle eyes trained on them and wondered if she sensed the undercurrent.

He tried to hide his acute interest in Lucy. After all, he'd sworn off women for a while. And she was sorely putting that commitment to the test. What was that verse that kept popping into his mind—"Test me, oh Lord, and try me." The Lord was doing a bang-up good job of it, and that was for certain. When he got home he was going to find out what the rest of the verse was so he could figure out a nice way to tell the Lord He could lay off. Lucy sitting next to him, at a crowded table, their elbows practically rubbing to-gether, and smelling of something fresh and sweet—Refusing temptation had never been his strong point. He had always gotten low marks.

His dad said the blessing, having come in just before the meal was ready, and Rowdy talked to the Lord and expressed his concerns. When he opened his eyes and glanced to his left, Lucy was looking at him—and for a second he got the feeling she'd been talking to the Lord just as fervently as he had about being forced to sit with him.

"You're an artist," Randolph said, after he finished blessing the food. It was more a statement than a question. "And you're tearing out and making a studio. How's that going?"

Rowdy had the feeling she'd been trying hard not to look at him up to this point.

"I'm getting all the ripping out done first before I start the rebuilding, though."

"Hopefully she's gonna leave some walls, but it sure is fun knocking them out," Wes called from his seat at the card table with Joseph and Tony.

"I'm leaving the major walls," she chuckled, and the sound had him fighting not to lean in closer to her.

"What do you paint?" Caleb asked, his big blue eyes full of curiosity.

"Well, I paint whatever catches my eye—people, flowers, whatever. But I'm known for roads and landscapes."

"You paint those yellow lines on the roads?" B.J. asked excitedly, and Rowdy was pretty certain the little kid thought that would be the greatest job in the world. Eight-year-olds saw the world in their own way.

"Not exactly. You see, I paint a road in a landscape." When it was clear he didn't understand, she added, "You know the gravel road that cuts through the pasture at the entrance of the ranch? Well, I'd paint something like that, when the bluebonnets are in bloom. Or the doves lined up on the telephone lines."

His brows crinkled up and Rowdy had to hide a chuckle.

"Why would you want to paint a road like that?"

She smiled, making Rowdy want to smile, too, because he was enjoying listening to her.

"Because I'm infatuated with them. I love roads and love pictures of roads that make people want to know where the road leads."

"But we know the one in the pasture leads here to the ranch," Sammy interjected, sitting up in his chair.

"But the first time you came here, did you know what was just over the hill? I mean, you could see the roof of this house, but didn't you wonder what the rest was going to look like? Weren't you curious what you would see once the car reached the top of the hill? Wasn't there a sense of wonder?"

"Yeah," Wes said, his voice trailing low. "I was hoping there would be a horse and, sure enough, there was one tied to the arena saddled and ready when the social worker stopped the car. It was awesome."

Lucy placed her elbows on the table and leaned closer. "Yes. That's what I love about a picture of a road—it lets the person viewing it dream their own story. Everyone who looks at a picture of a road sees and feels something different."

Rowdy got it, and his curiosity was ramped up to view her paintings. He liked the way her mind worked.

"I was hoping I'd find a place where I wouldn't be sent away." Tony's words rang through the silent room.

"And you found that, didn't you?"

His expression eased. "I found my family."

"And we are so glad you did." Nana said what everyone else was thinking.

"I think it would be neat to paint a picture," Sammy said. "Can we see some of yours sometime?"

"Sure. I'd love to show you when I get some unpacked. I don't really have much, though. What I've painted recently is at the galleries. But I've got to get busy because they are waiting on me to turn new work in. There's an important show coming up and I need something in it."

"I'd like to see some myself," Rowdy said, more than ever wanting to see her work.

"Sure," she said, their eyes meeting. Tearing his eyes away from hers, he gave his undivided attention to his pot roast. He liked his neighbor, it was true, but he had horses to train, boys to coach for the upcoming ranch-rodeo benefit and a cattle business to run at the same time. He had committed to helping sassy Lucy Calvert do a little remodeling, but that was it.

For now, anyway. He'd had the tendency to date women who were drama queens—partly because they were usually really good-looking and that seemed to be his downfall—not that he was proud of any of it, but he couldn't deny it. Maybe this attraction he was feeling toward Lucy was because she seemed to be the complete opposite of that.

He'd made a commitment to himself and the Lord. Women were off-limits. Until the Lord showed him the right woman, he wasn't making a move. No matter what.

"Lucy, I've been sitting here thinking and I've just had this crazy idea," Jolie said, leaning close to the table in her excitement and taking the heat off of Rowdy. "Would you consider teaching the boys a brief art class? Just a class or maybe two a week for five or six weeks?"

Startled by his sister-in-law's proposal, Rowdy swung his head to the side and saw that Lucy was just as startled. Then her eyes lit up as if she'd just been plugged into an electric outlet.

"I'd love to do that!" she exclaimed.

He held in a groan and knew right then and there that he was in trouble. "But you have your hands full of projects," he protested before he could stop himself. Every eye at the table slammed into him and he knew he should have kept his stinkin' mouth shut.

Test me, oh Lord—there was no denying it. None at all. God obviously got a real kick out of giving exams.

What had she just done? Lucy toyed with the collar of her shirt. She'd just committed to teaching the boys of Sunrise Ranch art lessons. The very idea sent shock through her, but excitement at the same time. She was going to teach an art class. And she was going to do it for these boys. It hit her suddenly that maybe this was what she was looking for. What she needed right now, a way to make her feel as if she was making a difference—her way of giving something back. Of paying it forward, so to speak.

This was her shot. It would be great!

"Whoa, there, you mean we're going to have to *paint* pictures?" The shock on Wes's face equaled that of being told he was going to participate in a ballet and it brought her excitement up short.

Cowboys obviously didn't do ballet or painting.

Joseph's eyes widened with worry, too. And with the two obvious leaders of the group balking at the idea, looks of excitement began giving way to looks of skepticism.

"Some of the greatest artists in the world are men," Lucy assured them, suddenly really wanting to do this. "Western art is a fantastic art form and I'd love to see if we have any future talent in this room with me."

Jolie jumped in to help. "Fellas, you'll have fun with this. Lucy and I will figure out projects you will enjoy. I promise."

Wes got a twinkle in his eyes. "I think if we have to paint, then Lucy needs to have to help us in the wild-cow-milking competition."

Excited chatter and agreements erupted about the room. Rowdy joined in the laughter beside her.

Well, she could have a good time, too. "Sure, I'd do that. I can learn to milk a cow."

Nana had been fairly quiet during the conversation, clearly enjoying listening, but now she chuckled. "Lucy, you're a good sport and true Sunrise Ranch material. But, to be fair, I think someone needs to explain the whole concept to you before you commit."

"That might be a good idea," Morgan agreed from across the table. "Jolie loves this sort of thing, but not all women do."

Instantly the competitive side of Lucy lit up. She might not be as tall and athletically built as Jolie, but she was certain that she could milk a cow. How hard could it be? "I'm sure it will be fun," she said.

"It is," Jolie told her. "Still, Wes, maybe you should explain this since it was your idea."

"It's a blast," the blond mischief maker said. "There's

a team of five and one of them is the 'milker' and one is the roper. While the other team members catch and control the wild cow, the milker gets the milk, then runs it to the finish line. It's a hoot and a half."

"Yeah, a hoot and a half," B.J. echoed. "You gonna do it?" His big dark eyes were wide with wonder and expectation.

Though Lucy had sudden qualms about the wild-cow part, she swallowed her trepidation and nodded. "Sure I am. I'm game for anything."

From the end of the table, Randolph joined the conversation. "For safety's sake, I'm going to venture in here and require you to have some experience under your belt before you jump out there and try it. Rowdy can be in charge of that. What do you say, Rowdy?"

Lucy's spirits sank like the *Titanic*. Suddenly she wasn't so sure about this great idea. She'd already allowed Rowdy to help with her construction. She'd realized tonight that she wasn't comfortable being in his company overly much. The man made her nervous—he affected her in ways that she'd rather not think about. Now this....

"Sure," Rowdy said beside her. "We'll figure something out."

It hit her that he didn't sound all that enthusiastic about the idea, either. As she turned to him, her arm brushed his. Tingles of awareness like an expanding spiderweb etched across her body.

"Good," Randolph said. "In that case, I'll look forward to seeing you in the competition."

"Sure." Lucy's voice was as weak as the smile she mustered up.

How had this happened?

B.J. tugged at her sleeve and she turned to him, glad to have a distraction from Rowdy. "We're gonna have fun." He dragged the word *fun* out for miles.

Lucy liked his positive thinking, but she wasn't so sure about that anymore.

Chapter Six

She'd awakened thinking of the man as if she had nothing else on her mind. She padded barefooted straight to the kitchen and the strong pot of coffee that she'd set to automatically brew this morning.

Yawning, she grabbed an oversize red cup from the cabinet and filled it almost to the brim. Taking a sip of the strong black brew, she let the warmth seep through her, then loaded it with three teaspoons of sugar—one more than usual for the extra shot of energy she would need before attempting to plaster a wall today. She took another sip, sighed then headed outside to drink it on the porch. She loved the quiet of the morning.

She'd come here to clear the air and move on with her life. Knocking walls out and spending her afternoons carrying the wood to a burn pile had empowered her. True, her back ached—and she'd had a very near miss with disaster—but since arriving in Dew Drop, she'd had a blast. And now she'd found something else to do that would be fulfilling—something she needed so badly.

Still, she knew it would take time away from her

own painting, which she really should get busy on as soon as she finished renovating. But she would make time for the art classes. They might actually help her regain that spark of enthusiasm she'd come here searching for.

She needed inspiration desperately.

Needed something to motivate her to pick her brushes back up.

She'd come here determined that if she got her studio just right, the joy would return. And she was still trusting that it would.

What about the cowboy?

There he was again, the big white elephant in the room. What about him?

Her cell phone rang, saving her for the moment.

Digging it out of her pocket, she glanced at the caller ID. So maybe she was wrong, she'd rather deal with the cowboy than her mom. Bracing for drama, she pushed the touch screen to accept the call.

"Hi, Mom."

"Have you lost your *mind?*"

"Not the last time I checked." Lucy concentrated on keeping her tone light, having long ago grown numb to the melodrama.

"Then why are you living at that dump in the middle of nowhere? You've come a long way, Lucy, after what that jerk did to you." Lucy held back a retort. Her mother had no room to call names, having put Lucy's father through basically the same thing that Tim had put Lucy through, only her mother had been an open book. But Nicole didn't see the two as the same thing; everything she did felt justified in her mind.

"Mom, we've been through this. I want to be here. I'm loving it."

"Your father should have stopped this—"

"I'm twenty-six years old and plenty old enough to make my own choices." *Without being dragged through guilt trips and hysterics.*

There was a long, exaggerated sigh on the other end of the line. "I never said you weren't capable of making your own choices." Nicole's voice dripped with emotion. "But what if *I* need you?"

And there was the whole gist of the conversation. Lucy fought off her own exaggerated sigh. "Mother, you are forty-seven years old—"

"Forty-four," her mother corrected.

Nicole had shaved off three years of her age a few years back. Just knocked them off and somehow didn't think anyone would notice. It wasn't worth arguing over. "The thing is, Mom, I moved here to start fresh. I am going to be fine and so are you. After all, you have Alberto."

"There you go again not paying attention to me. His name is Alonzo and no, I don't have him anymore."

Her mother was destined for unhappiness. The one good man she'd ever married had been Lucy's dad, and Nicole had kicked him to the curb years ago. And when Lucy's dad had had the audacity to fall in love and remarry—and be *happy*—Nicole had made it her life goal to try to make his life miserable.

Lucy had been the pawn her mother used most of the time in that quest. As a girl Lucy had suffered because of it and trusted no one with her heart until Tim. A bad move on her part—he and her mother were two of a kind.

"Mom, did you have a reason for this call?" Lucy asked, not happy about being reminded of what she wanted so much to escape.

She was ready to get to work and be done with this bad start to a good day.

"There you go being negative. Can't a mother just call to check on her child?"

Sure she could, but then Nicole wasn't a normal mother. There was always a reason for her call.

"Yes, she can." Lucy waited.

"Well, there is one thing," Nicole said, as if suddenly thinking of something. "Now that I've got you on the line. You still have your condo in Plano, right?"

"Yes." She hadn't put her condo on the market yet, wanting to make certain she wanted to stay here in Dew Drop.

"Great, then I'm sure you won't mind if I stay at your place for a while. I've moved out of Alonzo's place and…"

So that was it. "Yes, Mother. That will be fine. You know where the key is." And that was that.

Her mother made a quick ending to the call after she'd gotten what she wanted. Lucy held the phone for a minute, staring at it as she realized her bond with her mother was as blank as the screen. There was a time when she'd longed for more, but then she'd faced facts and knew it would never be more than it was now.

Standing, she looked about her new property. Her sweet uncle had wanted her to find that missing link here on this property and among the folks of Dew Drop. And maybe with her neighbors at Sunrise Ranch. He always had been a perceptive man.

Breathing in the fresh air, Lucy headed toward the

barn to find her sledgehammer—the hunk of metal had become her new best friend and she was smiling as she walked along.

Moose appeared, weaving between her feet and arching his back as he rubbed his furry orange body against her leg.

"You and me, Moose," she said, bending to tickle him between his ears. She had things to do. There was no time to waste on areas of her life she had no intention of opening up again.

Here she might have to figure out how to maneuver around her new neighbor, but her mother had just reminded her of the circus her life could be back home and what her uncle had known or hoped she would find on this property.

She could deal with a certain happy-go-lucky cowboy if she must in order to keep her feeling of contentment. Her mother could have Lucy's condo for all she cared.

What had he been thinking?

Stalking to the burn pile, Rowdy carried the guts of yet another wall that Lucy had decided needed to bite the dust. At this point he'd begun to really worry about the woman's brain. This wall wasn't connected to the living room/kitchen area or he would have put his foot down. This wall happened to be on the upper floor of the house between two small bedrooms that she'd decided needed to be one larger room. There was no doubt in anyone's mind that the woman liked open space.

Or, he had begun to wonder, perhaps she really did

just love to knock out walls. Maybe it was a disorder of some kind.

"Calamity Lucy's at it again," Wes said as he walked up. "I'm thinking we're going to have to talk her into leaving something standing in there or her house is gonna fall right on top of her."

"He might be right, Rowdy. Aren't you worried?" Joseph asked. "I mean, that's three walls. And I think she has her eye on the one beside her bedroom downstairs. I think I heard her muttering something about closet space."

Rowdy tossed his armload on the pile, stripped off his gloves and rested his hands on his hips. "I know it seems crazy, but it is her house, fellas. And to her credit, she hasn't knocked a wall out yet that would cause the house to cave in." For that he was grateful. He didn't tell the guys, but at the rate she was going it was only a matter of time before those were the only walls left, and then…who knew?

Wes rubbed his neck and squinted at Rowdy in the sun. "I guess it's good we're here to talk her off the ledge if she decides to get really crazy with the sledgehammer."

The kid had been ambling around nursing what looked to be a sore hip and a sore neck. Rowdy wondered again about whether he was bull riding. He'd asked about the hip and Wes had said he'd had a run-in with a steer. Logical answer…and maybe not the lie Rowdy suspected it was.

If his dad or his brothers suspected anything, none of them were saying. Maybe it would be better just to turn his head the other way and leave it be. As soon as the school year ended in six weeks, the kid was free to do as he pleased per the state. In all truth, he could do it now, but thankfully college was in Wes's plans.

Sunrise Ranch didn't cut the foster kids loose when the state did. Once they were here at the ranch, they were family and treated as such. Wes and Joseph were both graduating with scholarships to college. Joseph was heading off to become a vet and Wes was looking at an education in agriculture.

Rowdy pushed the thoughts away. He was probably worried about nothing. Looking at his watch, he saw it was nearing time for rodeo practice. "Hey, why don't y'all head back now? I'll go see if Lucy is ready to start practice tonight and be there soon. Tell Morg for me, okay?"

"Sure thing, Rowdy." Joseph nodded toward the house. "I think she might be a little worried about it."

Rowdy gave the kindhearted teen a smile. "I'll make sure she knows we're all going to take good care of her."

"I have a feeling she's tougher than she looks," Wes said. "Did either of you glimpse that burn on her neck?"

So they'd seen it, too. Since he'd seen it the other day, he was aware of it. He'd caught glimpses of it when she was busy working and forgot to tug her collar tight.

"I wondered if y'all had noticed," he said.

Joseph nodded. "I don't think she wants people to see it, though. Kind of like Tony not wanting to go without his shirt."

It was true. Tony had been badly mistreated by his parents before the state took him away from them and brought him to the ranch. His background was like nothing any kid should have to go through and he had scars to prove it. Bad scars that made Rowdy's stomach curl thinking about them.

"Maybe we can keep this between us, then," he said, immediately getting agreement from them. "I appreciate it, guys."

They headed toward the ranch truck as he headed toward the house. When he heard the distinct whack of a sledgehammer, he picked up his pace.

What could she be tearing out now?

Wes and Joseph's laughter followed him as he took the porch steps in a single stride and pulled open the screen door. Calamity Lucy they were calling her— he had to agree at this point. The woman had to stop. Getting her out of this house and involved in something else, even if it was wild-cow milking, was just the thing she needed.

Chapter Seven

"**O**kay, that does it. Put the sledgehammer down."

Lucy spun at Rowdy's irritated growl. "What do you think you're doing?" she gasped when he grabbed the tool. She hung on to the handle with all she had.

"I'm stopping you from destroying your house. Do you realize this is the *fourth* wall you've knocked out? Five, if you count the one in the barn."

"I can count, you know," she snapped. "And it's *my* house," she added indignantly, yanking hard on the sledgehammer. The irritating man yanked right back, slamming Lucy up against him with only the hammer between them.

"Let go, Lucy."

She glared up at him. "I will not!" The man had been working for her all afternoon and she'd been trying not to think about how every time he looked at her she forgot all about not wanting a man in her life.

Holding the handle with one hand, he covered her hands with the other. The work-roughened feel of them caused goose bumps on her arms.

His lip twitched at the corners as he stared down at

her. "You sure are pretty when your eyes are shooting fireworks. I'm kinda growing fond of it."

She couldn't breathe. She couldn't move. What had this man done to her?

One minute they were staring at each other, and then he lowered his head and kissed her. How dare he....

Goodness... The dreamy chant began ringing through her head as his lips melded with hers.

You're a fool, a fool, a fool, the small voice of sanity began to scream. Tearing her lips away from his, she put footage between them. "Why did you do that?"

His brows had crinkled together over teasing eyes. "I've been wanting to do it from the first day you dropped into my arms. And you know it. I've seen you looking at me, too."

Her jaw dropped. "You don't have a clue what I want. Or don't want." That he had her pegged did not make her feel good. "I don't want a man. I don't need a man. And certainly not one who kisses me right out of the blue like that." *Well, it had been nice—* She told the voice in her head to take a hike!

Rowdy stared at her as if she'd grown two heads or something. "Look," he said at last. "I kissed you. I'm sorry. I told you I was trying to mend my ways and you're right, I went and kissed you and I shouldn't have."

"Aha! So you freely admit that kissing women is a regular pastime for you. It just goes to show you that men are all despicable." The words just flowed out in a rush. "And another thing," she flung at him when suddenly it hit her that he was still looking at her as though she'd clearly lost her marbles.

She swallowed hard and prayed for the floor to open up and swallow her. How horribly embarrassing.

The clock on the wall in the next room could be heard in the silence that stretched between them.

"Are you okay?" Rowdy asked gently.

She couldn't look at him as she nodded.

"I'm really sorry. I overstepped myself and you're right. I was way out of line. It won't happen again."

He was actually apologizing to her. What a concept. When had Tim ever done that? Only when he'd wanted something…or when she'd figured out he'd done something he hadn't wanted her to find out about. The sleaze.

"Look." Rowdy held up his hands in surrender. "I'm not sure what your problem is, but if it will make you feel better, I'll leave." He turned to go and it was then that she realized she'd been glaring at him the whole time.

The man had to think she was a complete loon.

Stomach churning, she ran after him and caught him on the porch. The sun hung low on the horizon behind him. "Rowdy, wait. I might have overreacted."

At her quiet words he halted and turned back to her. "Maybe. But, hey, if my kiss drove you to it, then I guess that's a good thing. Only I get the feeling what's going on here goes a whole lot deeper than my kissing. Right?"

She owed him, so she nodded. "It's a long story."

"Look, I have a feeling you're not comfortable sharing whatever it is with me. Especially now. But how about getting out of the house to practice for the rodeo?"

She had to shut down the sudden impulse to spill

everything to him. Working with him was one thing—confessing to him was another. But she had made him feel terribly bad—at least it seemed that way—and she had signed on for this wild-cow milking. "Okay, that sounds like a plan," she said.

He waved a hand toward his truck. "In that case, your chariot awaits you. And I promise to stay on my side of the truck, behind the steering wheel."

Feeling more foolish than ever, Lucy pushed her hair behind her ear, contemplated changing her mind and then followed him to his truck.

"First things first. Do you know how to milk a cow?"

Lucy blinked blankly at him, and Rowdy took that as a no even before she confirmed what he'd figured out.

"Um, I can't say that I've ever had the need to know how to milk a cow."

Rowdy was having trouble concentrating. He shouldn't have kissed her. Hadn't meant to. He was a yahoo, a buffoon, an idiot. That was for certain. He'd swallowed the woman up as if she was sweet tea on a hot afternoon, and then he'd lost his mind in the process. He just didn't think straight around her.

He knew that now.

The thing was, he liked Lucy and he couldn't seem to do anything but want to get to know her better. But if he'd thought there was something bothering her before, he knew it was true now. Not that he was God's gift to women or anything, but she'd responded to him and then shoved him away as though he was Jack the Ripper.

What was her story? Something had happened to cause this leeriness.

She had a mistrust of men. And he wanted to know why.

The best way to do that was to get to know her, and teaching her to milk a cow was one more way to do that.

"So this isn't a milk cow." It wasn't a question but an observation on her part. She bit her lip—he fought to focus—and she studied the mama cow in the holding pen. "Aren't mama cows dangerous?"

"Yes, they are when their calf is around. They're not to be toyed with, and you need to know what you're doing so you can get in there and get out. Okay?"

She rolled her gorgeous eyes. "I'm thinking this is the craziest stunt I've ever agreed to."

He chuckled. "I hope so, because it is kind of crazy."

"Then why are you allowing the kids to do it?"

"They're ranch kids. Other kids skateboard on rails and jump bikes over holes and ramps. Ranch kids get in the arena with cattle."

She crossed her arms tight and glared at the cow that stood contently in the pen. He knew as well as she did when she started after the cow's udder things would change in an instant.

"Look, I don't want you to get hurt. The thing is the older teens know what they're doing. This isn't for little kids. You have to remember, one will have her head, and one will control her tail and one will be helping the boy holding the head. I'll be helping you get to the udder. They'll have her stretched out and it won't be as dangerous as it could be. You just have to look out for her feet, and I mean it. Watch them. Now I'm going to call the boys over and we're going to demonstrate."

"Fine. You do that."

He almost chuckled at the way she was fighting her fear. He'd learned that she wasn't one to back down.

Rowdy liked that. Respected it.

"Okay, you need to hold your hand like this, like you are going to shake my hand."

Lucy watched Rowdy hold his hand out with his fingers together and his thumb slightly separated from them. She copied him, trying hard not to think about the kiss. But it was a little bit distracting— Okay, it was a lot distracting.

She held her hand as he was and then looked skeptically at him. "Then what?"

"Then you grab here at the top," he explained. "No pulling like you see in the movies. Just clamp it between the fingers and push gently upward. Milk will come. Remember, in the competition, you need a few drops."

How hard could it be?

"And then you run."

She glared at him. "Thanks. Thanks for letting me get myself into this. If the boys don't want to paint, then I wonder why I'm doing this?"

"Sometimes even if a boy is curious about trying new things, he needs an excuse to do it. Painting isn't the most macho thing for these guys to do, so you getting in the ring with this cow gives them the excuse because you called their bluff. Get it?"

She did, actually. "Yes. So now I know." And she couldn't back down even if everything in her warned her to run now. As she looked at Rowdy, her stomach felt off-kilter and she wondered if the warning was for her to run from him instead.

"So do we have a regular milk cow somewhere that I can practice on?"

He chuckled. "Sorry, we're not in the milk-cow business. You're going to have to test it out on Betsy Lou here."

"Why does this not surprise me?"

"Hey, Wes, Joseph, y'all come on over." He'd sent the boys to practice with Morgan on the other end of the arena and now, at his call, the entire group came running. It looked as though she was about to be the show for the day.

Morgan rode his horse over behind the boys. She liked Morgan—he seemed to be a rock, and as steadfast as they came. She had a feeling—just from all the responsibility that he carried on his shoulders—that if a man could be trusted, Morgan McDermott would be that man. Rowdy's boyish grin tickled her memory.

Could Rowdy be trusted?

No. He was too reckless. Too good-time Rowdy. Not that anyone had told her this, but she knew in her heart that he was. Tim had had that same look. His smile came too easily and it teased too often.

The boys who weren't on the team climbed to the top of the arena rails. They looked so cute sitting up there. Wes, Joseph and Tony climbed between the rungs and sauntered her way.

"We'll take care of the cow," Wes said, looking cocky, and Lucy believed he would.

"We're going to let you learn here in the small pen. So I won't have to rope her, the boys will just grab her and then I'll move into place and tell you when to make your move."

She nodded. "Gotcha."

"Okay, then, let's get this party started. Fellas, it's all yours."

They whooped like she'd learned they were prone to do, then dived at the cow so fast it didn't have time to make a break for it. Wes grabbed the head and Tony joined him. Joseph grabbed the cow's tail. They all grinned at her as the cow let out a "Maaawwww" that sounded like a battle cry.

"Let's go. Follow my lead and watch out for the back leg. I'll get the milk first, so watch closely."

Was he kidding? She kept him squarely between her and the cow as she crept behind him. He whipped out the jar that was supposed to hold the milk, and as she watched he raced into the danger zone and reached for an udder.

It was *udderly* unbelievable. *Funny, Lucy, you're a real riot.*

"You do it like this," he called, bending toward the moving target. The boys were holding the cow, but she was bigger than them and not standing still. Rowdy displayed the milk in the clear jar as he moved back beside her.

"Piece of cake. You can do it."

"Yeah, go for it, Lucy!" the kids called from the fence.

Praying she didn't lose her lunch, she was so nervous, Lucy grabbed the jar and headed toward the cow with Rowdy beside her. "Piece of cake, my foot," she quipped, making herself smile for the kids. Hunching down, she reached toward the udder. When she slipped her hand in, the cow moved as she grabbed hold and milk shot her in the face.

Spitting and blinking, she scrambled to hang on. The cow bellowed and sidestepped, taking the boys with her. Lucy didn't let go, but lost her balance and fell forward, hitting the cow in the belly before planting herself face-first in the dirt! The cow bucked, kicked its leg out then stepped on her arm. Then her shoulder. Pain seared through her and Lucy would have screamed but her face was plastered two inches deep in smelly arena dirt.

Chapter Eight

This was not how it was supposed to go. Rowdy put himself between Lucy and the cow. The boys let the animal go and it sped to a corner at the far edge of the pen. Rowdy knelt down just as Lucy lifted her face out of the dirt and spat.

"This is *disgusting*," she croaked.

"Yeah, you're right. Sorr—" Rowdy's words stuck in his throat. The sleeve of her shirt was ripped and flapped open as she sat up, exposing her arm. The skin, as far down as he could see, was puckered and angry, disfigured terribly in spots. His gaze locked on her burn scar and he couldn't tear his eyes away. Suddenly seeing him looking, she snapped a hand to her arm and pulled the material closed the best she could.

Beside them, Tony stood stock-still, staring at her arm. Even though she now had it covered, it was clear Tony had glimpsed what lay beneath the cloth.

Rowdy moved to her side and helped her as she tried to stand up, not at all sure what to say. Her collar hung loose at her neck and the other scar was visible beneath. Without thinking of his actions, he reached and gently tugged the collar close to her neck like he'd seen her do so many times. Her eyes met his and there was no missing the pain shimmering in their depths.

"Thank you."

He nodded, his voice still lodged in his throat with the knot from his stomach. "Hey, guys, I think Lucy's been a good sport about this. We're going to call it even. Right?"

"R-right," Wes said. His blond brows dipped together and his expression revealed that he, too, had glimpsed the gruesome burn on Lucy's arm. "You just tell us where to show up for art class and we'll paint a road that no one will be able to forget."

That got a smile from Lucy. "We're going to start painting tomorrow. I talked to Jolie yesterday. But—" she grimaced, clearly in pain as she continued to grip her arm "—I'm going to compete in the rodeo just like I promised, so don't think I'm not going to hold up my part of the agreement. But right now I need to go home."

Rowdy shot Morgan a glance. "I'll be back."

"Don't worry about us. Make sure she's okay," Morgan said, frowning with concern.

"Yeah." Rowdy jogged after Lucy, who was already almost to his truck. He barely made it there before she did and pulled open the door for her. Without a word, she climbed in and stared straight ahead as he went around to his side. "See you fellas later," he called to the younger ones who were craning their necks from their perches, clearly worried.

"Tell Lucy she done good," B.J. called.

"I'll do that." Rowdy hopped behind the wheel and had them heading back toward her place within seconds.

She continued to stare straight ahead. When he glanced worriedly at her the second time, she swallowed hard and he wondered if she was fighting tears. If so, what did he say?

"Are you hurt? Those burns on your neck and arm look like they were painful." What an idiot. Clearly they'd been painful.

"They're well now. I think my shoulder is going to have a good-size bruise."

Her voice was soft. He had never been so glad to get to a house in all his days. He practically spun gravel turning into her driveway. He was out and around to her side of the truck before she had time to even think about opening the door herself.

"I'll see you tomorrow," she said, and headed toward her house, still holding her shoulder.

"Hey, I don't know what kind of men you're used to being around, but I'm not just going to drop you off alone after I got you stomped by a stinkin' cow."

She spun around. "I'm fine. I don't need your help."

What was with this woman?

"Of all the stubborn—" Rowdy stared at her, then marched past her to her front door. Yanking it open, he held it as she glared at him. "After you."

"Fine," she snapped, storming past him and through the door. "I'm going to wash my face and change my shirt—if that's okay with you?" Her eyes were like spikes.

"Fine with me. I'll be right here when you get back, and then we're going to talk."

Her brow shot up to her hairline. "Fine."

"Fine," he snapped, too, and watched her storm away. All the while his head was about to bust imagining all the different things that could have caused such a burn on her neck and arm.

Every one of those scenarios was too painful to think about.

They'd seen her arm. The look of horror on Tony's face had cut to her core. The kid had almost looked as if he could feel her pain.

Drats and more drats. Her scars made people uncomfortable.

She stared at herself in the mirror. It had taken a while for her to be able to do it without cringing, herself, so how did she expect others to not react the same way?

The brutal burn ran ugly and twisted from her neck down her right arm and torso. It wrapped around her rib cage and covered the majority of her stomach. The memory of the house caving in on her swept over her, and the scent of burning flesh made her nauseated. Reaching for the clean shirt, she pulled it on. The traumatic memory faded as she buttoned the buttons with shaky fingers.

Rowdy had seen the scar before and not said anything. Today, he'd looked into her eyes and pulled her shirt closed so no one else would see it. He'd saved her from the curious stares of the kids for the most part. Tony, and maybe Wes and Joseph, had seen her arm. He'd kept them from seeing more.

She had the feeling that this time he was going to ask questions.

Not sure if she was going to answer his questions she walked from her room and rounded the corner into the kitchen/construction site. Rowdy was leaning against the counter with his back to the sink and his scuffed boots crossed in front of him as he stared at the spot where she would be when she rounded the corner. She stopped. Her stomach felt unsteady…or maybe that was her feet. And her arm throbbed like a fifteen-hundred-pound cow had stepped on it.

As soon as he saw her he pushed away from the counter and yanked a chair from the table. "Here, have a seat."

She sat because she needed to.

He reached for a bottle of pain relievers that he'd obviously dug from her cabinet. Popping the top off he poured two into his hand and held them out to her. "You're going to need these."

She took them, because he was right. Then she accepted the water he held out to her.

Once she'd washed them down, he took her glass and set it on the counter, where he resumed his original pose leaning against it. His deep blue eyes rested on her.

The man really made her nervous.

"You were a good sport out there."

Not what she'd been expecting. "I still think y'all are crazy, but I'm going to do it."

"You don't have to. In the boys' book, getting out there and trying was all they needed."

"A deal is a deal."

They stared at each other and the clock ticked on the wall over the stove. "I guess you're wondering about my scars."

"I am. But if you want to tell me it's none of my business, I understand. You just seemed sort of—" He raked his hat from his head and ran his fingers through his straight dark hair. She could tell he was struggling with the right words. He didn't know that there weren't any.

She wanted to tell him it was none of his business but…he'd seen her arm. And her neck. Still, accepting them was one thing, but for her to talk about them was an entirely different one.

"Our house burned down. We were sleeping and didn't realize it until it was almost too late." Her heart rate kicked up and she rubbed her sweating palms on her jeans, while trying to control her breathing like the therapist had taught her. "The fire was hot and the smoke was so thick when we woke. Tim shook me awake, and we were crawling to the window when the roof caved in and burning wood rained down on top of us…" She hadn't told this much of the story to anyone but her therapist. "It was— I woke up in the hospital and they told me Tim hadn't made it."

She hadn't been able to talk about the moments of pain before she'd lost consciousness. Blinking back tears, she rubbed those that had escaped and were rolling down her cheeks. "I didn't know anything about Tim's affairs then," she almost blurted out, but didn't. She'd believed he'd died loving her. Even after she knew that was a lie, she wouldn't have wished death on him.

"I'm sorry." Rowdy came and pulled a chair out so he could sit facing her. He clasped her hands with his and squeezed gently. "That's tragic. All of it."

She nodded, closing her eyes. "Yeah, especially knowing I killed him."

Chapter Nine

"You killed him? I don't believe that," Rowdy blurted in reflex. He didn't know her well, but she hadn't killed her husband. No way.

She looked away, toward the window that could be seen past the breakfast bar in the front room. "It's true. The fire started in my studio with some oily rags."

Guilt was etched in her features when she turned back to him. "That may be the case, but you didn't start the fire. Things happen. I'm sorry you lost him that way." He could tell she took what he said with a grain of salt. She looked to be around twenty-five or twenty-six. About his age.

She'd been through a lot for her age. He didn't know a lot about art, but he thought he knew making money in the art world was almost impossible. So there was one more thing to be curious about.

"You must have loved him very much." His heart ached for her—having lost his mother at a young age, he knew the pain that went with losing someone you loved.

She lifted a shoulder in a slight shrug. She stood

suddenly. "Hey, thanks for bringing me home. But I need to get some things unpacked for art class tomorrow."

"Sure," he said, knowing a dismissal when he heard it. "You're sure you're okay? Do you need anything?"

She shook her head. "Nope. Really. I'm good." She had begun walking toward the door the moment she'd started speaking. He followed like a puppy being sent outside. She opened the door and held it for him. He ignored the urge to touch her as he walked past. He'd been pretty harsh earlier, and now he felt like a heel.

She didn't follow him onto the porch.

"Take another couple of those painkillers before you go to bed," he said, as if the woman didn't know how to take care of sore muscles.

"I'll do that. Good night."

Before he got his good-night out, she'd already closed the door. He stared at it, stunned. Something tugged in his chest. And he wondered for the umpteenth time what had happened to Lucy Calvert. There was more to this story. He felt it to his core.

He didn't feel right leaving. He raised his hand to knock but let it hover just in front of the door before pulling back. Turning away, he strode to his truck and left.

Lucy had a right to her privacy.

Lucy couldn't believe she'd opened up to Rowdy about the fire. She'd had to catch herself before she said too much. And yet she'd admitted the part that tormented her. Yes, she was angry at Tim for what he'd done. But to know that she was responsible for a person losing his life... It was unthinkable.

And then there was the scene at the burn center. His girlfriend blaming her and the horrible things she'd learned that day.

Lucy poured herself a glass of iced tea and drank half the glass, suddenly feeling parched as a desert. Then, forcing the thoughts away, she headed to the back room where she'd stored her canvas and paint supplies. It was time to think about something positive. Teaching the boys to paint appealed to her. She'd never thought of teaching before, but with this wild bunch, she was certain it was going to be an adventure.

And that was exactly what she needed.

Did it matter that they'd seen her scars? She would see tomorrow. Tony would have time to let the shock of seeing them ease and they'd move on. No big deal.

No big deal.

Rowdy's soft gaze touching hers as he'd pulled her collar closed slipped into her thoughts. The man had been nothing but kind to her since she'd arrived—bossy and nosy, too, but kind. Her lips lifted thinking about him. Why was a guy like him still single? The question startled her.

She had come here so angry at Tim. At herself. And here was this handsome cowboy who wouldn't go away. Of course, she could say he was just being neighborly… but that kiss had nothing neighborly written in it. Tracing a finger along the edge of an unfinished canvas, she remembered his kiss, and the feel of it came surging back and almost took her breath away.

No, neighborly was not what she'd call that kiss.

Chemistry, yes. Very much so.

And it had been a very long time since she'd felt anything like that. For two years her life had been full of pain, inside and out. Her extensive burns hadn't been a simple fix.

God had been good to her during that time. She didn't think she could have made it through without Him, but God hadn't been able to fix the anger inside of her. He hadn't been able to fix the mistrust that ate at her.

But tonight, she'd talked to Rowdy. Opened up to him in a way she hadn't been able to do with anyone since she woke in the hospital, other than her therapist at the burn center.

She'd trusted Rowdy enough to do that.

The very idea was a breakthrough for her. Maybe God had brought her here for that reason.

Taking a deep breath, she began assessing supplies she would need tomorrow. Jolie had taken the list of paints she'd need to the art store in the larger town eighty miles away and had promised to pick up some canvases, too. Despite feeling nervous about tomorrow after all that had happened today, she went to work gathering the rest of the things she would need.

So far life here at her new home hadn't been anything like she expected, not quiet time spent alone rehabbing her house and her soul— Nope, not that at all.

Rowdy, she had to admit, was the most unexpected. Trepidation filled her again when she thought about having opened up to him. She hadn't told him about the scars on her body. Had let him think the scars on her arm and neck were all there was. Why had she done that?

She knew why she hadn't said anything about Tim's cheating for so long. It was embarrassing. But was that why she'd kept silent about the scars?

* * *

"Tony, dude, you saw how bad they were, didn't you?" Wes, Tony and Joseph were sitting out under the crooked tree back behind the schoolhouse. They'd agreed to meet there after practice, after seeing the scars on Lucy's arm. The younger boys hadn't been close enough to see them.

Tony nodded. "They were bad. Like angry welts."

"Like yours," Joseph said, looking sad.

Wes knew Joe had a tender heart. It was one of the reasons he was going to make a good veterinarian. Wes wasn't as tenderhearted. He got plenty mad when he thought about his life, but he stuffed it deep inside of him and for the most part enjoyed his life here on the ranch. He felt lucky to be here. Looking at Tony, he knew his life could have been rougher. At least his parents had just left him on the steps of the welfare office. They hadn't tortured him like Tony's parents had.

They hadn't tossed gas on him and struck a match.

"Yeah, like mine. I wonder what happened to her?"

"I don't know, but she's hiding them," Wes said.

Tony looked down, rubbed his hand on his thigh. "It's easier that way," he said, real quiet. "People look at you funny. Y'all know it. Y'all've seen the look on people's faces the first time they see my back. It ain't worth it. I totally get why Lucy covers hers up."

Wes did, too. It was true what Tony said about people getting all shocked and horrified at the sight of his back. His back looked like roadkill. He didn't hardly ever go without his shirt.

They were all quiet for a few minutes. It was hard to say anything after something like that.

"I'm just glad you didn't die from it." Joseph was the one to speak.

"Yeah." Tony took a deep breath. "Truth is, till I came here to Sunrise Ranch, I kinda wished it had… you know. Killed me." He swallowed hard and chucked the rock he'd been holding as far as it would go.

Wes figured he had it good compared to Tony, but then he still didn't get why a kid had to go through all the junk the world had to offer sometimes.

Tony smiled and changed the subject. "Did—" He started to say something, then stopped. "Did you see the way Rowdy looked at her?"

"You mean with the goo-goo eyes?" Wes grinned.

"I saw it," Joseph said. "It's pretty clear he's into her. I mean, I could tell that when we were working at her place."

"Yeah, I know," Tony said. "But did you see how he didn't care about the burns?"

Wes shot Joseph a glance. They stopped grinning.

"Not everybody's going to freak over your burns, either, Tony," Wes said, hoping he was saying the right thing.

"Yeah, maybe." Tony shrugged, looking as though he didn't believe it.

Wes's fist knotted up and he had to knock the anger back in its dark hole. "You hold your head up, dude. It'll happen."

"Yes, it will," Joseph added.

Wes sure hoped so. He wondered if Lucy had the same thoughts as Tony. "Maybe Rowdy will fall in love with Lucy, you think?"

A grin spread across Joseph's and Tony's faces.

Yup, that would be the cool…and it might make Tony feel better about himself. That would be the coolest of all.

"Y'all did great today," Lucy called, forcing her voice to sound upbeat as the kids streamed through the schoolhouse door like a herd of wild mustangs. Several shot thanks over their shoulders, but nearly pushed the others down clamoring to get away.

Lucy sighed, watching the last one escape. Her shoulders drooped; it had not exactly been the day she'd planned.

"They love working cattle, so don't let their stampede out of here get you down," Jolie said, coming up beside her. "You did great, and I think they enjoyed themselves."

"Like a trip to the dentist."

Jolie chuckled. "It wasn't that bad. And remember, they're boys. When you get more to the actual painting part of the class things will get better."

"Well, at least there's hope." It was true that today she had to spend time teaching a little theory. Not much, but she had to explain the different art forms, the brushes and mixing the paint, etcetera.

"I'm pleased. They need a little Art 101 and it's just a wonderful thing that you showed up right here beside us. God just works everything out. It's a wonderful thing to watch."

It was Lucy's turn to chuckle. "I'm not so sure the fellas would agree."

"They don't have a clue what's good for them." Jolie winked and then began straightening desks. Lucy did the same. "So how's the remodel going?"

"Pretty good. I think we've got all the walls knocked out that I can possibly knock out."

"Well that's a good thing. I overheard something about Calamity Lucy the other day. We're studying women of the West right now and so they have heard stories of Calamity Jane. I think they were beginning to fear the house was going to fall in on you."

She shook her head. "Crazy guys. I do admit that I kind of fell in love with certain aspects of swinging that sledgehammer. There's a lot of clearing of the head that goes into that swing."

Jolie sat on the edge of the desk as her smile bloomed wide. "Speaking of Rowdy, how's that going?"

Had they been speaking of Rowdy? She thought they'd been speaking of her house and clearing her head. Suddenly uncomfortable with the conversation, Lucy bluffed. "What do you mean?"

"C'mon. There's something there. I saw it the other night. It's okay. I can tell you he's a good guy."

"First of all, I'm not looking for any kind of guy right now. Just so you know. But also, he told me he's trying to mend his ways. That's a red flag to me. I bet he's very popular." *With the ladies* went unsaid.

"And I'll be one of the first to say he needs to mend his ways. Especially after..." Jolie's words trailed off and her eyes dimmed.

Lucy didn't want to pry, but couldn't help herself. "What? After what?"

Jolie bit her lip. "I shouldn't have said that. Rowdy is a great guy. I've known him since I came here at age ten, when my parents were house parents. He didn't take his mother's death well. He got into all kinds of trouble—reckless stuff. My mom used to say it was as if his mother dying young made him think his life was going to end early, too, so he might as well live fast and furiously. He almost got killed trying to ride a bull that the best bull riders in the country had trouble riding. It stomped him—it was terrible. It scared Randolph to death." Jolie shook her head. "Anyway, I know we all want the best for him."

Jolie had changed what she'd been about to say, but hearing about Rowdy as a grieving boy tugged at Lucy's heart. Still, why had Jolie thrown out the "especially after" comment, then backpedalled like an Olympian?

Whatever it was, she'd already figured out it couldn't be good or Jolie would have had no reason to withhold from her.

"Rowdy just needs someone who can help mend the heart of that boy he once was. By the way, I want to say how sorry I am. I read the article about the fire." Her eyes softened. "I'm sorry you lost your husband and were so badly burned. A terrible thing. I guess me pushing you about an interest in Rowdy is probably way off base right now. Forget I said anything. I'm just glad you're here and agreed to teach art to the guys. Working with them will bless your soul."

Lucy tried to figure out what to say, but in the end she said nothing. Just that the boys already were getting to her in a good way, and then she'd gotten out of there as fast as she could.

She had very nearly let her defenses down where Rowdy was concerned. The thought plagued her all the way home.

There was something behind Jolie's remark. And it had a big red stop sign painted all over it. And yet, she thought about that boy who lost his mother and dealt with it by living hard and recklessly, and her heart ached for him.

Chapter Ten

Driving back from Bandera a few days after Lucy had told him about her husband, Rowdy had a lot of time to think. He'd been unable to get her off his mind. He'd had to make the almost four-hour trip to hill country on the spur of the moment to finalize the buying of a horse he'd been working on for weeks. The trip had turned into a two-day affair and he was anxious to get home.

Morgan had relayed to him that the first two art classes had been exactly as they'd all thought they'd be—met with strong opposition.

"If it had been us being forced to lift a brush at that age, we'd have been moaning just as loud," he'd told Morgan.

"You'd probably have skipped out and found you someplace to hide out there holed up under the stars where you always used to run," Morgan had accused, and been right on target.

Still, that being said, he hoped the boys weren't making Lucy feel too bad.

He had to admit that after hearing her story—or at least part of what he suspected was a story with more to it—he was glad Jolie had asked her to teach the art class. It opened up a reason for her to be at the ranch some. He knew that what he and the boys could do at her house was not going to last much longer. They'd already knocked out every wall that could be knocked out and the hedges were all trimmed and the yard cleaned up. He enjoyed being around Lucy. He couldn't deny it.

He was supposed to be cooling his jets, and here he had gone and kissed the first woman since "the bad move of the century." The only good thing he could say about that—other than the fact that he'd enjoyed it more than any kiss he'd ever experienced in his entire life—was that at least he'd kissed a good woman. A really good woman.

Not that every woman he'd ever dated had been bad—they were just not what he was looking for anymore. He was digging himself deeper and deeper. He was a shallow jerk.

It was as much his problem as it had been theirs. Until Liz.

Liz was in a realm all her own, and if there was one good thing he could say for her, it was that at least knowing her had set him on a different course. He still felt for her family and what she'd put them through. And he knew that when and if he ever married, he was taking no chances on a woman like Liz standing across from him saying "I do."

Like his dad had said, there was always a positive to every situation. You could learn from the bad ones and if you didn't, then the blame for that sat squarely on your own shoulders.

Rowdy had learned and learned well.

His dad had also told him once that living hard

wouldn't bring back his mother. Wouldn't right the wrong he'd felt done to him when she died. They'd created the ranch as a haven for lost boys, boys who had no one and yet Randolph sometimes worried that Rowdy was the most lost and alone of all the boys who'd come to the ranch. Rowdy couldn't do anything more than just look at his dad that day, because he'd felt his words were true.

Staring at the night flashing by, Rowdy wasn't sure why his thoughts had gone there. He didn't like excuses, didn't like thinking that he had been unable to deal with the feelings of loss that had coiled inside of him for so long. He'd been angry on the inside—hiding it as best he could—finding relief in his reckless ways.

Much as he suspected Wes was doing. For Rowdy, everything had come to a jolting halt when he'd been confronted by Liz's husband. It was as if icy cold water had been poured over him, startling him awake.

He'd known then he wanted to change. He'd gone down on his knees and asked the Lord to forgive him. To change him. And that change was in process.

He just hadn't refined the process yet. Bad habits were hard to break. Especially when a gal like Lucy fell into his arms.

He smiled thinking about that first meeting. She'd surprised him from the beginning, and every day he wanted to know more about her.

Not far to go until he'd be driving past her place. It was late, but if her lights were on, he might stop in.

Once again, maybe he was getting ahead of himself.

Patience had never been a strong suit of his.

So he'd play it by ear. It was eleven o'clock, anyway.

She was probably snug in bed with the lights off. The best thing he could do was drive on by and let her be.

Lucy stared at the sketch she'd just finished of how she wanted the studio to look. The barn was sturdy and the concrete slab made it all the more workable to have an art studio here in the loft. Sitting on the edge of the loft with her legs hanging over instead of her body this time, she studied the floor below. There were possibilities for that space, too…if what she'd heard at the Spotted Cow Café today had been any sign. Both Mabel and Jo had voiced a desire to learn to paint. They'd said they had a lot of friends who would enjoy an art class one night a week—maybe even two.

Possibilities. She let her imagination open and saw the loft as her personal studio with the first floor set up as an art classroom. The idea wasn't something she'd even thought about until Jolie had asked her to teach the boys. What a disaster that was on the verge of being. But if she was actually offering art classes to people who wanted to take them, and were excited about it— Well, that was really appealing to her.

As far as the guys, she was feeling like a failure, despite Jolie assuring her they'd come around.

Ha!

The crunch of tires, then headlights flashing across the open barn doors, alerted her that someone was pulling into her driveway. She glanced at her watch. It was after eleven-thirty.

Who would be coming to her house at this late hour?

And what was she doing out in the barn this late alone? Her door was even unlocked and every light in the house was on. *Hello—*

She'd not realized how late it was. She'd gotten lost in her drawing. Pulling her legs back from the edge, she stood and went to the window to peek out and see who was out there.

Rowdy!

What was he doing here so late?

She'd been relieved when he hadn't shown up to work two days ago. The boys had relayed the message that he'd had ranch business out of town. It hadn't made her happy that her first reaction had been to feel let down that he was gone. She'd kicked that out the door in an instant and been more than happy not to have to see him for a few days. It gave her time to think. Time to take control of her circumstances again.

She'd called a contractor and set up a meeting for tomorrow.

Rowdy got out of his truck, stretched and then, looking better than she wished he did, he strode to her back door and knocked on the screen-door frame.

Drats!

He waited, looked at his watch then turned and glanced toward the barn. She knew he couldn't see her and she didn't move. But then she realized that maybe since it was so late, there was an important reason he was out there.

"Rowdy," she called, pushing the window open and waving. "I'm up here. Is everything all right?"

"Lucy! What are you doing out there at this time of night?"

Okay, so maybe she should have let him stand out there all night. "I'm working. What are you doing?"

"Looking for you?" He was steadily heading toward

her. The barn's spotlight showcased him all the way. He looked up as he got closer. "Mind if I come up?"

Yes. "No," she said instead. Walking over, she sat back down on the edge of the loft and let her legs dangle as she watched him stomp up the stairs.

When he made it to the floor he came and sat down beside her. Too close for comfort, his shoulder brushed hers. Butterflies came out of nowhere and attacked her stomach. There were just some things she was finding out that she couldn't control. Butterflies were one of them.

Drat and double drat!

God had been having an excellent day when He'd created Lucy Calvert. Yessiree, it was true. He'd also been on a let's-torture-Rowdy kick.

He'd missed her.

There, he admitted it. Staring into those amazing eyes, he knew there was no use trying to deny it.

"What did you say you were out here doing? Working?" he asked as the sounds of the night settled in the stillness between them. Through the open barn doors, crickets chirped and he could hear the coyotes in the distance, so far off their lonesome call almost blended with the night.

She nodded, picking up a sketch pad on the floor beside her. She handed it to him. His fingers brushed hers as he took it. "This your studio?" he asked, trying not to send any signals that would put a wall up between them.

She'd had her hands folded together in her lap, and now she just nodded. This had been a bad idea on his part. But to be true to the path he'd committed to with the Lord, he was keeping his distance.

Looking into her eyes, he knew he was a fickle soul. That had always been his problem where women were concerned. But if he didn't want to run Lucy off, then he now understood he would have to move slowly. She was different than any woman he'd ever known.

He yanked his gaze away from hers and stared at the drawing. He sent up a prayer for help.

Because he did have good intentions.

"Yes. I drew it up and kind of lost track of time. The contractor starts on Monday."

She'd hired a contractor. He'd known this was coming, had thought as much earlier, but he knew that meant his time here was done. He hadn't realized it was going to hit so hard. "So you're kicking me and the boys out?"

"Y'all have been wonderful, but a girl can't wear out her welcome. You have a job to do and the guys have enough on their hands with school, ranch work and preparing for the rodeo."

It was true.

"Besides, I only agreed to let y'all help for a short term. And my agent really needs me to get busy."

True again.

"You're sure this doesn't have anything to do with me grabbing you like a jerk and kissing you?"

She stared up at the rafters for a moment, engrossed in the moths playing in the lamplight as she stalled for time.

"Maybe some. But you have been nothing but great to me since the moment I moved in here. It's me. There's—" She stopped speaking and took a deep breath.

He waited.

"I didn't tell you the whole story the other day."

You haven't told her the complete story, either. "Look, about that. I need to say something here," he said.

She shook her head. "No. I need to tell you something first. I think you deserve to know so you understand."

His gut burned with the need to come clean. It was as if once he'd realized Lucy deserved to know, he needed to get it out. But ladies go first. "Okay, then you first."

"I've told you that my husband was having an affair when he died. It's hard to think about, much less talk about."

Lucy's expression was so mingled with anger and sorrow he wanted to put his arms around her and comfort her. But he couldn't move.

He caught himself before blurting out that her husband was an idiot. "Who in their right mind would do that to you?" He finally said what he'd been thinking ever since she'd first told him about her husband's cheating.

She wrapped her arms together across her midriff and held his serious gaze with one of her own. "Tim Dean Calvert, that's who."

Tim Dense Calvert. "So were you still together when the fire happened?" he asked, wanting to know more—he'd felt from her first revelation that there was more to this story. She'd said they were asleep. So she'd overlooked the affair. That didn't strike him as the Lucy he knew.

"I didn't know. I found out afterward."

"Afterward. So were you having problems?" What was he pumping her for information for? *Did you love the guy when he died?* The question slammed into him and he held it back.

"Not as far as I knew. Well, some. Things had gotten tense. But you know, that happens." She took a deep breath and stared at the clouds as if seeking her next words. "I woke up and found I was in a burn center and my husband was dead. I was grieving when…the next day a woman came to my room."

He didn't like the way this story was going at all.

Her eyes glittered. "She was bitter and blamed me for the fire that had killed the man she was in love with. She told me about the affair and that Tim had planned to leave me for her. I mean, honestly, how could I have been so blind?" She took a deep breath but he couldn't find words.

"Once I got out of the hospital, several friends came to me and told me they'd known of Tim's infidelities. *Infidelities.* As in more than this woman. But they hadn't known how to tell me…so they'd said nothing."

Rowdy started to speak but she picked back up as if once she'd started talking she couldn't stop.

"I haven't looked at anything the same since. So many things came to light about the real Tim that I had to take a good hard look at my life. I think I knew deep in my heart something wasn't right, but I just hadn't wanted to face it."

The look on her face told him she'd begun to question herself in that time. He couldn't even imagine how horrible that had been for her. Burned as bad as her neck and arm were, and the pain she must have been in both physically and emotionally. And that was before being confronted by the other woman.

"Unbelievable," he said at last. "That explains the walls." It all made perfect sense now.

And he was toast.

She shivered though it wasn't cold. "Yes, it's been two years and I'm still angry. But coming here has been good for me. And those walls, though great therapy, haven't been completely satisfactory in ridding me of the anger. Or my other issues."

"Other issues?" *Please, Lord, don't let her have gone through something else.*

She looked almost apologetic. "You've been nothing but nice to me, but I can't get past the broken trust. I don't know that I'll ever trust a man to get close to me…ever. I think you should know that since I reacted so badly the other day."

Burned toast. Rowdy rubbed his jaw, completely understanding Liz's husband trying to break it with his fist. Rowdy would have found great satisfaction in breaking Tim *Dense* Calvert's jaw.

"And now that you know, you'll understand why I'd like you to not kiss me again."

His blood was rushing in his head so fast he was dizzy. "Sure," he managed. Any chance he might have thought he had with Lucy was gone. Period. If she found out about what he'd done, she'd probably hold it against him.

"Now, what were you going to tell me?"

"Aah, I… It's not important." God forgive him but he couldn't tell her. Not right now. She suddenly looked tired, defeated and he just couldn't add more on top of that—at least that was his excuse to keep his mouth shut.

"Then I think I'll call it a night."

"Yeah, me, too." He needed to get out of there.

He stood up and took her hand, tugging her up and away from the edge, not taking any chances she was going to tip over. There was that same electrical voltage sparking from her to him but he played cool, letting go the minute she was safe.

They walked one behind the other down the steps and across the yard. His mind was racing and guilt kept trying to suffocate him. "I'll see you later," he said, stopping at his truck.

She turned and walked backward a few steps. "Yes. Later. Good night."

And then she spun around, hurried up the steps and disappeared through the door without another glance.

Toast. How had he ever been so stupid? He had a horrible feeling that the best thing that had ever happened to him had just walked out of his life.

Chapter Eleven

The music was already playing when Lucy walked into the side door of the church—a rustic-looking building set on a hill overlooking the town. She'd been planning to visit ever since she'd arrived, but had found herself dragging her feet. Today she knew she needed to be here. Dew Drop had a couple of churches, but Nana had told her this was where they worshipped, and so she'd come to visit. She'd stayed home the first couple of Sundays in town, settling in. It was a lame excuse, she knew, but since her life had turned upside down, she'd only gone to church sporadically. She'd had anger issues to deal with. She wasn't angry with God, but with Tim. She was determined to put that all behind her. She prayed that God would ease the knot that had buried deep in her heart.

The interior of the church was different from most, also rustic looking with concrete floors and cedar walls.

Mabel and Ms. Jo were the first to greet her.

"Lucy, it is good to see you here." Mabel hunched down and engulfed Lucy in a hug. The overpowering scent of magnolias clung to Lucy even after Mabel let go of her.

"You'll learn to run when you see her coming," Ms. Jo said, eye to eye since they were both less than five foot. "Mabel, she's blue. Do you see that? One of these days you're gonna let loose of someone and they're gonna already have gone to their heavenly reward."

Lucy chuckled, trying to breathe past the magnolia fumes stuck to the white blouse she was wearing with her slacks. "I'll live, so rest easy that it won't be me," she said, tugging her collar close, making sure it was in place. "I'm glad to see y'all." It was so true. They'd been so nice coming out to the house and welcoming her.

"Then come on over here and sit with us." Mabel locked her arm through Lucy's and started walking her toward the pews that were set in rows. Lucy almost had to run to keep up with Mabel's long strides.

"Dragging the poor girl around like a rag doll," she heard Ms. Jo grunt.

Mabel ignored her as the band of men with guitars up on the platform stood and began strumming. "We've been hearing good things from Ruby Ann, haven't we, Jo?" Mabel pulled Lucy into a pew in the middle section.

"Said Rowdy's become a regular over at your place." Ms. Jo pushed her round glasses up on her pert nose, her intelligent eyes seeing right through Lucy—or at least that was how it felt.

"That's what she said, all right. He's a wild one, but worth taming, if you know what I mean."

Lucy wasn't sure she wanted to know. And she was about to say there was nothing personal between them when the band let loose with a foot-stompin' version of "I'll Fly Away."

Ms. Jo went to clapping and Mabel did, too—thankfully she'd let go of Lucy's arm. Now that she was settled, she realized that the band consisted of Mr. Drewbaker Mackintosh playing a guitar. His pal Mr. Chili Crump was getting after it on a fiddle. There were a couple of other young cowboys playing guitars that she didn't recognize. The lead singer, though, she thought worked for Sunrise Ranch.

With Mabel and Ms. Jo settled in enjoying the music, Lucy relaxed. She looked around and saw the boys lined up in two rows. B.J. was sitting beside Rowdy, looking at her. He lifted his hand and gave her a small wave.

She smiled at him, then went back to watching the band. She didn't want Rowdy to catch her looking at him. The last thing she needed was for him to think she was staring at him. He sure did look nice in his crisp burgundy shirt and starched jeans. Her gaze wandered back to his direction when the band started playing George Strait's "I Saw God Today."

Ms. Jo caught her looking and grinned. "Don't you just love Cowboy Church? A little traditional mixed with our cowboy culture. That George is telling the truth in this song. All you have to do is look around to see God's working miracles everywhere."

Lucy did not know exactly what to think of that statement. She had a feeling she was talking about more than the song itself.

When the band ended and the preacher stepped up to the podium, she had to force herself to concentrate and not let her mind wander across the aisle to Rowdy.

She'd opened up to him about Tim. It wasn't something she talked about. But once she'd started telling him the whole ugly story, she couldn't stop. Maybe it was simply because she'd made him think the kissing freak-out she'd had was his fault, when she'd known it really wasn't. And maybe it was because she was attracted to him and he was attracted to her and he needed to know the boundaries. It was only fair.

She was facing things straight on now, or at least looking at life with her eyes wide-open. No more sleeping on the job for her. She did not need a man in her life. She didn't need the headache of always looking over her shoulder. She had Tim to thank for that.

Her gaze slid to Rowdy again. His dark hair lay smooth at the nape of his neck and almost touched his collar— *What was she doing?*

Lucy yanked her gaze away and stared at the preacher. She concentrated on what he was saying.

"...Psalm 147 says, 'He heals the brokenhearted and binds up their wounds.'"

Lucy couldn't move; the words were so relevant for her. As if the Lord had been listening to her heart.

But it wasn't that easy for wounds to heal.

Beating down walls was far easier than letting go. Her gaze shifted back to Rowdy, who had yet to glance her way as far as she could tell. She'd told him to leave her alone when it came to a relationship. Made it perfectly clear and he'd agreed on the spot. Her wounds were too deep to completely heal.

Just too deep...

Sunday after church, the arena was full as the boys practiced for the ranch rodeo. He wasn't sure if Lucy would show up, given that she'd been kicked during the first practice and then there was the uncomfortable situation he'd put them in with the kiss. And then there was his past and her past and the fact that there was not going to be any meeting in the middle.

Their situation ate at him. He hadn't been able to get the fact that there seemed no solution to help their relationship out of his mind. He'd gotten up before daylight and started riding the new horse just because riding and thinking went hand in hand for him.

But it hadn't helped him much this morning. Lucy was a hard woman to figure out, and she'd been through more than any woman should have to go through.

He let her have her space at church that morning. He was glad she was there. When the service was over, he'd stopped by where she was talking to the boys and reminded her of practice in case she wanted to come. He'd had to force himself to look at her. After the preacher's sermon about wounds and how God could mend the brokenhearted, he'd started praying that He would do this for Lucy. But he knew it would take time. And even then with his past, there was no hope.

They'd been practicing for about thirty minutes and there was no sign of her. He hated it, that he'd made her uncomfortable…that he'd messed his life up and that the consequences of his past stood between them like a mountain.

"Lucy's coming!" Sammy called, riding his horse over to the fence and waving his coiled rope in the air as Lucy's black Dodge pulled to a stop beside the arena.

Rowdy's chest felt like a steel band had just clamped down around it, and he forced himself to hold back. Morgan rode up beside him.

"Looks like it's your lucky day," he said, smiling.

"Yeah, I wish. She's out of my league, bro."

"Well, that's true, but sometimes that doesn't matter. Jolie picked me."

He knew Morgan was trying to make him feel better, but Morgan hadn't done the things he'd done. Morgan had always been a hardworking class act—yeah, he'd been irritating as all get-out growing up, but it was true. Rowdy had been the wild child, living recklessly and choosing unwisely. He was just thankful that God hadn't let go of him through all of his prodigal-son days.

Regret was a hard companion, though, and despite having his life on track, it trailed him like a bloodhound.

Lucy was smiling and kidding with the boys as she climbed to the top rail of the arena. She wore her long-sleeved shirt and her stiff collar. Her beautiful hair cascaded around her shoulders. Her smile was contagious.

Feeling like a stack of horseshoes was stuck in his throat, he rode over and forced a grin. He might not have a future with her, but he could be her friend.

"So are you here to watch or are we going to have another go at it?" Okay, not the best word choice.

"I'm here to milk a wild cow." There was challenge in her eyes. "That was the bargain I made with the fellas."

"We don't want you gettin' hurt." Wes came out of a holding pen where he'd been helping B.J. learn to wrestle a small calf. "Ain't that right, little dude?" he asked, scrubbing B.J.'s head with his knuckles. B.J. grinned and twisted away, laughing as he ran over and climbed up the fence to Lucy.

"We don't want you to get hurt, but if I can learn, I know you can, too. It's fun. You shoulda just seen me take that calf over there down. I mean, I locked him in a headlock like Wes just done me, and that dude came right off his feet. You should try that."

Lucy had started smiling halfway through the boy's excited words. He was standing on the rungs with his hands on the rail behind him, grinning at her. She smoothed his hair out of his eyes and Rowdy's admiration of her went up yet another notch. She got that these boys craved love from the adults around them. The small kids especially needed the attention of the women who were in their lives.

That he was jealous of her gentle touch was understandable. Only a fool wouldn't want to get close to Lucy, so at least he recognized that he had grown smarter over the past little while.

"You know," he said, a thought hitting him. "B.J. has a good idea. Learning to wrestle a calf would be good for you. It would help you with your reflexes and make you more comfortable being around the cattle."

She looked at him for the first time. He felt the spark of electricity that arched between them all the way to the tips of his boots.

"I'll do whatever you cowboys think I should. You may make a cowgirl out of me yet."

"It won't be hard," Joseph said, grinning affably. "If you just change your sledgehammer skills over to cowboy'n, you'll leave us in your dust."

That got hoots, and she made a cute face at them all.

"Then let's get to it," Rowdy said, needing action rather than sitting in the saddle mooning over what he couldn't have.

Send For
2 FREE BOOKS
Today!

I accept your offer!

Please send me two free novels and two mystery gifts (gifts worth about $10). I understand that these books are completely free—even the shipping and handling will be paid—and I am under no obligation to purchase anything, ever, as explained on the back of this card.

❏ I prefer the regular-print edition
105/305 IDL F479

❏ I prefer the larger-print edition
122/322 IDL F479

Please Print

FIRST NAME

LAST NAME

ADDRESS

APT.#   CITY

STATE/PROV.   ZIP/POSTAL CODE

Visit us online at
www.ReaderService.com

◄ Detach card and mail today. No stamp needed. ◄ © 2013 HARLEQUIN ENTERPRISES LIMITED. ® and ™ are trademarks owned and used by the trademark owner and/or its licensee. Printed in the U.S.A.

Send For
2 FREE BOOKS
Today!

I accept your offer!

Please send me two free novels and two mystery gifts (gifts worth about $10). I understand that these books are completely free—even the shipping and handling will be paid—and I am under no obligation to purchase anything, ever, as explained on the back of this card.

❏ I prefer the regular-print edition
105/305 IDL F479

❏ I prefer the larger-print edition
122/322 IDL F479

Please Print

FIRST NAME

LAST NAME

ADDRESS

APT.#   CITY

STATE/PROV.   ZIP/POSTAL CODE

Visit us online at
www.ReaderService.com

LI-1/14-GF-13

▲ Detach card and mail today. No stamp needed. ▲ © 2013 HARLEQUIN ENTERPRISES LIMITED. ® and ™ are trademarks owned and used by the trademark owner and/or its licensee. Printed in the U.S.A.

* * *

Climbing from the top rail, Lucy felt glad. Sitting there trying not to stare at Rowdy had been hard. But the boys were so sweet and she was determined to make them proud of her.

Wrestling a calf sounded perfect. At the moment, she had so much pent-up frustration about the entire situation that her life was in she could probably milk a wild cow and wrestle a bull at the same time.

Of course, she thought a little late, after she was already in the pen with the calf and Rowdy, that she was doomed. Goodness, her senses were in overdrive standing there beside him.

"Okay, I'm going to hold him. What you need to do is lock your elbow like this." He held his arm crooked to illustrate.

"Like Wes had me," B.J. called. "You just don't give the calf a knuckle to his noggin."

Lucy laughed despite her nerves. "Okay, I'll remember that."

"Once you have him like that, lean back and he'll flip with you. A bigger calf is going to be harder but if you put your determination into the elbow lock and twist he's going to do just what you ask."

Looking up, she got lost in his eyes. Her throat cramped and she couldn't speak. She nodded instead and ripped her gaze from his and back to the calf.

"I can do this," she said, accepting the challenge. Wanting the challenge. "I don't need you to hold him."

"Show him you're the boss."

A roar of agreement went up from the boys gathered tight around the pen.

She laughed hesitantly and shot Rowdy a glare. It

was his fault after all. The man smelled of leather and something so tantalizing she wanted to lock him in a neck hold. What was she thinking? "I've got this."

He grinned and waved an arm. "Go for it," he said, backing out of the way to lean against the fence panel, arms crossed and a too-cute-for-words expression on his face.

She took a step toward the calf and suddenly there was no standing still. The animal bolted toward the fence, faked left then turned right. She went left and landed in the dirt. A roar of laughter erupted behind her. Gritting her teeth, she was up in a second. The animal might be small but it was quick. Something bigger might have been easier than this. But she was not going to let it get the better of her.

It raced past her again and she grabbed its head, tripped and was suddenly being dragged around like a rag doll. How embarrassing was that?

Letting go, she was once more on the ground looking at the underbelly of the calf as it jumped over her. Rolling over, Lucy managed to grab its tail as it flew past and off they went. Hanging on, her ears ringing, her teeth chattering, she spat dirt as she sought to pull her feet around and get them back under her. She almost had her feet under her when the calf kicked a hoof back—Lucy let go in reflex and the foot missed her by a breath.

"It's okay, Lucy. You got nothing to be ashamed of."

She glanced at Sammy with his skinny face and big brown eyes. "Honest. I didn't know how to do that, either, 'bout six months ago."

"Thanks, kiddo," she grunted, pushing up from the

dirt. Rowdy reached down and took her elbow, helping her up.

He was grinning. "You've got gumption, that's for sure."

"Is that what it is?"

"Yup. It's a respect builder. And you've just earned some stripes." He winked at her and suddenly Lucy felt ten feet tall.

As she looked around at the fence Wes and Joseph gave her a thumbs-up. Tony followed and then all the boys copied all the older guys.

Taking a deep breath, she pushed her hair out of her face. "I guess Rome wasn't built in a day."

"Nope." Rowdy let go of her elbow, his hand coming to cup her chin. Her heart kicked. "You have dirt—" He gently brushed his fingers beneath her right eye.

All the air in the universe stalled at his touch. "Thanks," she said breathlessly.

He let his hand drop, looking suddenly as if he'd just been caught stealing money from the benevolence fund. "Sorry. I forgot," he said for her ears only, and stepped away.

Forgot what? Oh…that.

So had she!

Chapter Twelve

The diner was crowded Monday morning as Rowdy and Morgan made their way inside.

He'd come to town to pick up feed and met Morgan coming out of the post office. They'd decided to stop for a piece of pie—it was hard to pass up and Rowdy needed to talk to Morgan anyway.

Weaving their way to a table, they shook hands with several regulars as they went. Drewbaker and Chili were sitting at the first booth. They had the *Dew Drop News* spread open over their coffee mugs.

"Hey, hey, McDermotts," Drewbaker said, pointing at his plate of pie with his fork. "Try the chocolate. It's extra nice today. Jo was feeling particularly generous with the cocoa when she whipped these together."

Chili nodded as he stuffed a forkful of it into his mouth. "Good stuff," he mumbled.

"I'm convinced." Morgan chuckled.

Rowdy looked back at Chili as they slid into the booth at the back. "Don't choke on that." The older man hiked a brow and plopped another forkful into his mouth in answer.

"So what's your poison?" Edwina the waitress asked, coming to stand beside their table. "Food or dessert first?" Edwina had the coarse voice of gravel in a grinder and the dry humor to match.

"No 'how do you do' or anything?" Rowdy teased. "My feelings are hurt."

"As they should be. This smile of mine has been known to cause men to faint," she drawled. "I finally understand why all three of my ex-husbands just lay around the house during our years of matrimonial torture—they'd passed out from my smile. And all that time I mistakenly called them lazy no 'counts."

Morgan and Rowdy both grinned. Edwina hadn't had the best record with men. At least she could joke about it.

"You're probably right. No need to smile on our 'counts," Morgan said.

"Yeah, I've got horses to ride when I get home," Rowdy added. "No time for passing out, so it's just as well you keep your frown firmly planted downhill."

She tugged her pencil from the crease of her ear. "You two always were the smarter ones— Well, I take that back. Rowdy, you've still got some catching up to do. But I'll tell you what. If I decide to tag a fourth husband to my belt, I'll give you first shot. How's that sound? And Tucker already turned me down, just so you know."

"Well, Ed, that sounds like a plan. In the meantime I'll have coffee and a piece of the chocolate pie the boys recommended. And I'm wounded that you made the offer to Tucker first."

"Hey, he's the law around these parts. It was just

smart thinkin' on my end. But he's passin' on my beauty. Morgan, what about you?"

"Ed, are we still talking marriage or pie?"

She gave her lopsided grin that took up most of one side of her face. "You're taken already, so we're talking pie."

"Then I'll have the same as Rowdy."

"Back in a jiffy."

When she was gone Morgan asked, "So what's the story with you and Lucy? If I had just suspected something was going on, it was made perfectly clear in the pen with the calf yesterday."

Rowdy leaned in. "I messed up. I kissed her."

There was a heavy pause as Morgan let the words sink in. "So that's it. It's plain you two have a connection."

"It was a stupid thing to do. She's had it rough and—" he shifted uncomfortably "—with my past, when she learns of it, I won't be her fondest friend. As it is, she's had it so rough that trusting a man is the last thing she's going to do and one who just hauls off and kisses her? Big mistake." He kept his voice low. There was no way he wanted anyone else hearing what he had to say. Talking about this in the diner was a mistake.

"I'm impressed."

Rowdy was not in the mood for jokes, and the glare he shot Morgan said as much.

"Hey, I'm serious. You obviously have some good emotions going on for Lucy if you're this concerned. That's a good thing."

"I'm not so sure about that. I'm supposed to be changed—to be moving slowly where women are concerned—and here I up and kissed her."

Edwina walked up with their pie and he leaned back again and tried to look relaxed.

She gave him the eagle eye as she placed the plate and his coffee in front of him. "You look like you ate a porcupine while I was gone."

"You got that right," he said, giving her a half-hearted smile.

"Eat this pie and all your troubles will disappear. If they don't, take it up with Ms. Jo." She shook her head and walked away to bring words of wisdom to the next table.

Rowdy cut a big bite of the chocolate pie and let the rich flavor give him some comfort as he mulled over the situation.

Morgan did the same. After a few minutes, Morgan said, "Don't beat yourself up. Women are just hard to read sometimes. But there's something going on here, or it wouldn't matter to either one of you. Give it time. You're making progress, and don't forget that."

Rowdy drank his coffee, his mind tumbling over itself thinking about Morgan's words. Progress. Was he?

He hoped so.

But there were some things even progress couldn't help.

The contractor had started working on her studio and had informed her that the barn had good sturdy bones. He'd have the loft finished in a couple of weeks.

Wonderful!

Or at least it should be, but she wasn't in the best of moods. Lucy hopped to her feet. She had to get outside; a walk would do her good.

There was only a mild breeze blowing across the

endless pastures as she started walking. Moose pranced behind her, stalking grasshoppers along the way.

The sky was a gorgeous cerulean-blue, the clouds perfect for painting. Despite her foul mood, the walk seemed to clear out some of the negativity and she was not quite as down as she made her way back up the hill thirty minutes later.

To her surprise, Tony was sitting on her back porch playing with Moose, who'd abandoned her not long after she'd started the walk. When he saw her, Tony jerked to his feet.

"Hi, Lucy."

"Hey, yourself," she said, feeling better just seeing him.

He looked nervous, she realized. "Is something wrong, Tony?"

He sat back down on the porch and Moose curled against his side. "Can I ask you something?"

"Sure." Lucy sat down on the other side of Moose.

"I saw your scars the other day."

Lucy took a long breath. She'd never talked to him and Wes and Joseph about seeing her scars. "I thought so."

"You know I have them, too."

The words took her by surprise. "I'm sorry, I didn't know."

He was such a handsome kid and he now pinned serious eyes on her. Pain was shining in them. "My parents... Anyway, I've been thinking about it and watching you. And I figured out you're not comfortable with them. Me, either, just so you know."

She didn't know what to make of this. Why had he come? She looked around to see how he'd gotten there and spotted a horse tied to the fence. It was almost hidden by a huge oak tree.

"It's been bugging me, and I had to come make sure you knew you weren't alone."

Lucy blinked back the threat of tears. Tony was concerned for her. How bad were his scars? she wondered. And she was afraid to know how he got them, realizing that he'd almost said something about his parents. Surely not from them?

"Thank you for your concern. I'm so sorry you've suffered, too. And you're right that I'm shy about them. They—" She started to say they made people uncomfortable, but how could she say that without telling him his scars did the same? The thought of this kid being handicapped by the fear of others seeing his scars just didn't sit well with her. She couldn't do it, so she changed her words. "I was burned two years ago."

"I was ten—when I came here and it stopped."

Lucy's stomach turned. *It stopped.* What did that mean?

He stood up. "Anyway, just came by to say that I enjoyed your classes."

Lucy's heart clutched. "You did?"

He nodded and gave her a half grin. "Don't tell the fellas, though. You know—" he shrugged "—I was thinking it might be cool to paint something on the ranch. There's some pretty places here. I figure some of the others might like that, too."

She smiled and suddenly felt like crying with happiness. "Thanks for telling me, Tony. About everything. And I think I can get us to paint a ranch scene."

He nodded, ducked his head and headed for his

horse, and within moments was riding across the pasture toward the ranch.

Lucy watched him go. "Moose," she whispered. "I have an art class to prepare for."

And she had questions that needed answering.

Hopping in her truck, she headed down the road toward Sunrise Ranch, feeling so sorry for Tony but also like the sun had just risen. She knew how to get the boys' attention now. Classes were going on over at the school; Jolie's cranberry-colored Jeep sat out beside the building. Lucy parked her truck in front of the Chow Hall and met Randolph coming out the door.

"Hi, Lucy. Everything going good?"

"Hi, I was looking for Nana. Is she around?"

Randolph looked apologetic. "Sorry, she went grocery shopping. Is there anything I can help you with?"

Rowdy's dad was a handsome man with a great smile, like him. He had silver temples and coal-black hair otherwise. From what she'd learned of him, his wife had passed away before her dream of opening the ranch up as a foster home became reality. Randolph and Nana had worked hard to make her dream happen and, all these years later, he was still devoting his life to better the lives of all the boys who had come and gone. And he'd never remarried. For all the trust issues she had, she couldn't help but admire him.

"I bet you can. I'm sure you've heard that art class could be better, but I have an idea about that. I need some places on the ranch where we can take the guys and let them paint in the open. Something really great to hold their attention. Can you give me some suggestions?"

"I think that's a great idea." He looked thoughtful for a moment. "But the man for this job is Rowdy. Why don't you head over there through the stable to the round pen? He's working a horse. Rowdy knows this ranch better than all of us. He can show you some spots and then you can go from there."

It was inevitable—once again Rowdy was the answer. And besides, she needed to talk to him about Tony.

She'd tried for the past few days, since the roping, to not think about him but she hadn't succeeded. He'd snuck into her thoughts every time she let her guard down.

"Thanks, I'll head over there now."

"He'll fix you up," Randolph said, and headed toward his truck.

Lucy crossed the yard and walked into the stable.

"Hi, Lucy," Walter Pepper called from inside a stall where he was brushing down a black horse.

"Hi, Mr. Pepper. I'm looking for Rowdy," she said. He grinned and pointed toward the doors on the other end. "Thanks."

The scents of hay and feed tickled her nose as she went, and the anticipation of seeing Rowdy tickled her stomach.

The round pen was just out the back with Rowdy inside astride a beautiful horse. Tan with a black mane, the animal was as handsome as the cowboy riding him.

As he concentrated, Rowdy was at an angle to her, and while she could see his face in profile she knew that he hadn't seen her. She leaned against the side of the stables and watched, mesmerized.

The horse made a quick maneuver forward, then cut left, then right. The movements would have tossed

Lucy out of the saddle and straight into the dirt. But Rowdy was almost like a part of the horse, and not only stayed in the saddle but in control.

Lucy knew enough about quarter horses to know in a real-life situation there would be a calf or cow breaking for freedom. The horse was trained to cut in front of it and get it to go where he wanted it to.

She knew Rowdy had made a name for himself in a competition setting with several of the ranch's quarter horses. Unable to help herself, she'd looked him up on the internet and had been stunned to see how successful he was.

He'd never mentioned that. Never said anything other than that he ran the cattle operation of the ranch.

She wasn't sure how long she watched him before he saw her. And her heart betrayed her when it jumped the instant his gaze touched hers across the round pen railing.

Beefing up her determination, she gave him a small wave. "Hey."

He walked the horse over to where she stood. "This is a surprise. I hadn't expected to see you."

"Yes, well, I need your help." *Keep it about the boys. This doesn't have to be personal.* "I need you to show me some places you think the boys would like to try to paint."

He just stared at her for a minute. "Okay," he said at last. "Give me a minute and then we'll load up."

The butterflies that had been hibernating since she'd last seen Rowdy came alive—and the way her pulse was pounding it felt as though each one of them was working a sledgehammer.

"Sure, sounds good." She managed to hold her voice

steady despite the construction site her insides had suddenly become.

Truth was, turning around and running back to her place sounded much better. Much safer.

Much, much safer.

Sunrise Ranch was made up of ten thousand acres, and they leased another ten thousand from surrounding landowners. It wasn't the King Ranch by any means, but it was a manageable size and a beauty.

He'd offered several options when he and Lucy had first climbed into his truck. The river, the valleys— What did she have in mind? She'd said for him to show her his favorite places because places that touched one person would touch others.

There was nothing personal in her voice when she said the words. It was business. Sure. At least she was speaking to him. That was a positive. She might not want him to kiss her, but she didn't seem to mind being around him. That was good for now. He didn't know how long that would last.

"There will be lots of things to see on the way to the spots I've got in mind," he'd said. "So if you see something you like, just let me know and we'll stop and check it out."

She had a camera with her. And a sketch pad. She'd nodded and they'd been on their way. Neither had said much since then and it had been a good twenty minutes. He was afraid of opening his mouth too soon and her telling him to take her back to her truck. At least this far out it was a safe bet that she'd not want to try walking when he made her mad.

Not that he was going to do that intentionally. Nope,

he was keeping this conversation as nonrisky as possible.

She'd been sitting over there hugging the door, as rigid as a T-post. But now her shoulders had relaxed and she had settled back into the seat a bit. It was hard not to relax when driving across the ranch. The ranch had always given him a sense of peace. Even when he was at his most reckless, after he was in his teens and the anger at his mother's death had steeped for a few years, riding the ranch had been the place where he could think. Where he could almost feel God's touch.

It was that peace and beauty that his mother had loved. That she'd wanted to share with less-fortunate kids. He knew that was why he'd found comfort roaming the land his mother had loved. The kids… Back then they had been a major issue for him. He'd been a kid who'd lost his mother, and then suddenly he was forced to share his beloved ranch with other kids. At first he'd had trouble. Thankfully, he'd gotten over that within a year.

"This is gorgeous."

He almost jumped when she spoke. "Yeah, I think so."

"This is a great time, too—all these spring flowers in bloom. After the drought two years ago, I love seeing them again."

"Me, too." The drought had not only stressed the ranch out financially with the lack of grass but had also forced a sell-off of livestock in order to trim expenses down to a minimum. But the damage it had done to the land had been hard to stomach. Thankfully this year there had been a decent amount of rain and the wildflowers were a sign that things were on the mend.

"Stop!" she exclaimed as they rounded a curve on the barely visible ruts they called a road. In front of them, the road made a wide arch and then disappeared over the ridge. Wildflowers of a variety of colors with vivid splashes of pink and yellow jumped out at them.

Overhead, an eagle soared.

"You have eagles." She scrambled from the truck and started shooting photos in rapid fire.

Rowdy stayed watching her as she moved in front of the truck, then across to the side, taking shot after shot.

He wished he had a camera. Then, remembering he did, he grabbed his cell phone and started snapping pictures of her.

When the eagle soared over the ridge and finally disappeared she turned, smiling as wide as the eagle's wingspan, and came back to the truck and climbed in.

Rowdy's heart hammered like the staccato of a horse racing across a wooden bridge. She was beautiful.

Whoa, boy!

"Yeah," he said, his voice tight. "Let's get over that ridge and see what you say."

"I say that's a wonderful plan. I'm dying to know where this road goes."

Roads. Right. She painted roads…. He knew what was on the other side of the ridge, but for a moment he wondered where this road led, too. The one he and Lucy were on together. Maybe there wasn't any hope for him, but like Morgan said, he was making progress. Their road led somewhere.

"I love this spot," Lucy said a few minutes later, as she looked out over the rugged terrain. Once they'd topped the ridge, the wildflowers had diminished but the road turned into gravel, and the soft pink of buttercups and wild lavender verbena trailed through the scattered rocks along the road that sloped downhill to the base of a rocky ravine. Like a wall before them, the ravine rose up, and at the top a gorgeous, huge dogwood was in full bloom. Mid-April was the perfect time of year, and the dogwood wouldn't last long. Beauty was fleeting. But not for Lucy; he knew her beauty, her goodness, radiated from the inside.

He wondered if she even realized how beautiful she was. He wondered if she worried about her scars. He wished he could help her see that they didn't matter.

"It is breathtaking and manly. It might appeal to the boys. Can we transport art class out here tomorrow?"

He jerked his mind back to what she was saying. "Sure. Whatever you want."

"This is just to encourage them. We'll start out with background and slowly build from there with each lesson."

"Sounds good to me. I can't say I've ever painted, so I don't have a clue."

"Then you should join us."

He relaxed against the fender of his truck, watching her, and shook his head. "I'm not an artist. I want to see your work, not mine."

"You might surprise yourself. There could be a masterpiece or two inside of you."

He grinned. "I don't think so. My place is on the back of a horse."

"And you do a beautiful job of that. I enjoyed watching you work with that horse earlier."

That she'd said that pleased him. "Thanks."

She smiled, gave a nod and then, as if realizing suddenly they were staring at each other, she looked up at the dogwood. "I love what a dogwood stands for," she said. "God's love is so deep. My grandmother used to always tell me that the white color represented Jesus's purity. The four leaves represented His hands and feet and the burgundy indents on each leaf represented the blood He shed for us." She looked at him then, strong yet gentle.

"My mom used to tell me something similar. I think that's one reason this is the perfect place for the boys to paint."

She smiled. "They need every reminder we can give them that they are not only loved by us, but by God."

Rowdy's heart was banging again. This time it was because she got it. She got everything about Sunrise Ranch and the mission of it. "Yes. Exactly."

She sobered suddenly. "Rowdy, Tony came to see me this morning. I don't know if he skipped class, but if he did, I hope he didn't get into trouble. He needed to tell me something."

"He's a good kid. If he felt compelled to come see you, I know it was for a good reason. He won't be in trouble."

"Good. He—he came and told me he was burned, too. He told me he didn't want me to feel alone." She shook her head and swiped a tear from her cheek. "How could parents hurt their child like that?"

Rowdy wanted to hug her so badly he could barely stand it. "It happens every day," he said, his voice gruff. "It makes me furious, but I've come to realize that here on this ranch we can help heal their hearts. This is where *I* can make a difference. And that helps me. You're making a difference, too. Tony doesn't talk about his past much. So I know your scars are tough for you…but God just used them to touch a kid."

Her eyes filled with tears and she shook her head. "No, God used that beautiful, brave kid to touch me, too."

Chapter Thirteen

Using a few two-by-fours nailed together, the men constructed several easels for the kids' canvases, and Lucy watched as they loaded them in the back of the truck. Rowdy had hooked a trailer to the truck and threw some hay bales on it, and the boys were ready for a hayride across the ranch.

Lucy was pleased that the boys seemed more excited about the whole process.

"You mean I'm gonna get to paint a rock today. Not a flower?" B.J. asked the question with the serious eyes of an eight-year-old. As if painting a flower would give him cooties.

Jolie and Lucy both laughed at his seriousness. A rock rated very highly on his radar.

Lucy couldn't help reaching out to tousle his hair. "Yes, you will be able to look at the landscape I've chosen and focus on a rock if that's what you'd like to paint the most."

"All right!" he yelled, doing a jump and running off to grab Sammy's arm and give him the great news.

Jolie reached for another canvas to load on the trailer. "Kids—the funniest things make them happy."

"I know," Lucy agreed, carrying the case with the paint to the trailer. "I'm thrilled this outing is making them more excited."

"They just love being outside. And besides, they really were worried about you after you got kicked by that heifer. And then when you came back and held your own with that calf, you should have heard them talking about how you wouldn't give up. They like you, Calamity Lucy."

Lucy rolled her eyes. "They're really calling me that?"

"Just in teasing," Wes said, overhearing her comment. He was helping Rowdy load a cooler full of drinks. "Your house just barely missed imploding. One more wall and poof, down it would have come."

"I have to agree," Rowdy said. "The boys were thinking of confiscating the sledgehammer."

Lucy rolled her eyes. "Y'all are crazy. Jolie, they knocked out five walls. There are at least five still standing." She laughed.

Nana came out of the Chow Hall, followed by Joseph and Tony carrying another large ice chest. They'd already loaded one just as big.

"There's enough food in those two chests to serve an army, so you should be okay. And the third one Wes and Rowdy brought out is packed full of water and sodas."

Lucy went over and gave her a hug. "Thanks, this is going to be a good day."

"Me and the girls are champing at the bit to do this.

Have you thought any more about offering us old fogies art classes?"

"I have, and the contractor started yesterday. The place is going to be finished very quickly. It's nothing elaborate, more a rustic-cottage style. And if y'all are really interested, then I'd love to start a class and see how it goes."

"Wonderful! I'll tell the gals. They are going to be excited."

"I'd be interested, too," Jolie said. "It would be a great girls' night out."

Lucy was touched. "I'm getting more excited by the minute."

"Okay, load up," Rowdy called.

Morgan and Randolph had come out of the office.

"Have a good time," Morgan called to the boys. He slipped his arm around Jolie's waist and hugged her to his side. "This was a very good idea."

"Yes, I think so. Lucy's a gem for doing it."

"My pleasure."

Randolph had been talking to the boys who'd rushed the hay wagon. "Settle down when the trailer is in motion. I don't want any of you falling off and getting hurt."

Every one of the boys listened to him and stopped their good-natured pushing and shoving.

Rowdy grinned. "That's more like it. Okay, let's go paint us a rock." He shot a wink at B.J., who giggled and pumped his arm in the air.

Jolie and Lucy climbed in the truck with Rowdy and, since Jolie beat Lucy to the truck and claimed the backseat first, that left Lucy in the front seat with Rowdy.

Thoughts of him had hovered in the background of her thoughts since yesterday, and she wasn't pleased about that.

He'd agreed not to kiss her anymore and clearly had taken his hands-off promise seriously. But yesterday when she had gotten emotional talking about Tony, she'd wished he had folded her in those strong arms of his and held her close. Instead, he'd remained firmly where he was, and though his words were comforting, his arms had stayed locked tightly across his chest.

What was wrong with her? She'd gotten what she wanted, so she should be relieved.

But she wasn't. So far today he'd stayed on the fringes as they'd gotten everything loaded up. She thought he'd say he was dropping them off and coming back later to pick them up. But that wasn't so. Jolie had wanted one man out there with them since they were going to be a good distance from the compound. With this many crazy boys, they needed a man along.

Lucy was in agreement, but had half hoped Morgan would be the one to go. Or one of the many cowboys who worked at the ranch. But no, it was Rowdy and she was stuck.

Stuck in the middle of so many conflicting emotions, she felt dizzy.

She didn't want to put herself out there. She didn't want to put herself at risk again in a relationship. No matter how much she was beginning to wish she could each time she looked at Rowdy McDermott.

"It looks like a fat tick sitting on a pile of mud," Wes said, standing back and staring critically at his painting.

Rowdy had to agree with the kid. He hid a grin.

"Now, Wes," Lucy said, coming to stand beside the teen. "You've actually got some very good undertones in this. Now you need some variation of tones. Listen, guys. Brown is not simply made up of brown. If you'll look over there at that rock cluster for a minute, I'll explain again. See the way the sun glints off it? It looks lighter in that spot, right?"

Wes grunted what Rowdy took as a yes. And others agreed.

"To get that take your brush and dip it in the light ochre color, that's the yellowish color that I had you place on your palette. Then add it onto the rock like this." She demonstrated a quick dash on the rock and suddenly there was a little definition to Wes's tick.

"Hey, that's weird how it looks better."

Lucy chuckled, looking up at Wes. "It's really fun to see how different colors create what most people look at and see as a single color. That rock is made of lots of tones. Now you try it. Wipe your brush and add another tone. Mix a couple of tones together to make a completely new shade. Go have a close-up look at mine and see the various strokes."

Excited calls for help had her moving to the next kid, and she gave him her undivided attention. Rowdy enjoyed watching her in action.

Lucy was kind, and her goodness came across when she was dealing with the kids. He still couldn't understand her husband. How could a man do that to such a wonderful woman? It went against everything Rowdy believed in. He might not have dated wisely before but he could honestly say he believed in marriage. When he married, he'd be committing for life. And he was going to be looking for a woman of good character when he fell in love.

"You sure are in deep thought," Jolie said, coming to stand beside him.

"Hey, Pest, I'm a deep thinker. Haven't you figured that out after all this time?" He nudged her arm playfully. Jolie had grown up with them ever since she was about ten. And he'd been calling her Pest from day one.

"I totally have. So you like her a lot, huh?" She always had been too perceptive.

"What's not to like? But I'm afraid my past might be too much for her to handle. And with good reason. Some mistakes aren't fixable."

"Everyone deserves a second chance. You certainly do."

He slid a skeptical eyebrow up. "I don't know. Maybe, but it may not be something Lucy can accept. After hearing her story, I get it."

"You're all right, brother-in-law. Maybe time can merge your stories." She started to walk away, then turned. "She told you her story and that counts for something. Don't forget that. She shared some things about her past that she doesn't just share with anyone, so that's a good thing. Remember anything worth having is worth being patient for."

Patience. It was going to kill him.

Lucy was happy that the day was going so well. At noon they paused, and she and Jolie opened the ice chest and pulled out the lunch that Nana had so carefully created. The woman knew how to feed the masses, that was for certain. There were thick roast turkey sandwiches, sandwich bags full of homemade brownies and pound cake, plus chips and dips and cut vegetables. The woman thought of everything. And no telling how many hours she'd spent preparing the fare for "her boys," as she called them all.

"Your grandmother is amazing," Lucy said, when Rowdy came to stand by her and watch as the boys raided the open ice chest like ants.

"Tell me something I don't know. She loves it. Lives for it actually." He looked thoughtful. "It's kind of weird, but this was my mother's dream, and when my dad took up the flag and carried it, Nana just took to it like it had been her destiny all along. God has a plan, doesn't He?"

Lucy stared at him, dumbfounded. "Yes, He does."

He looked a little uncomfortable. "Do you want to take a walk over there and eat on the trailer?"

The boys were sitting around on the ground with Jolie and asking her some questions about kayaking. The trailer was empty. "Sure," Lucy agreed.

He grabbed a couple of sandwiches and a couple of waters, then handing one each to her, they walked over to the trailer.

They both concentrated on opening their sandwiches and taking their first bite.

"Delicious." Nana could cook. The sandwich nearly melted in her mouth, it was so tender and juicy.

He just nodded and took a bite himself.

After a few minutes spent enjoying half the sandwiches, he nodded toward the paint setup. "This is good for them. Jolie had a great idea. Thanks for doing it."

She took a deep breath, studying the boys, then turned to him again. "They are so funny. And I'm loving it. You know, what you do is wonderful, also.

Teaching them to work cattle and have fun at the same time. It's a good thing, Rowdy. You said the other day that this was where you could make a difference and it's true. You are." She meant it, too. Rowdy's attitude, his ability to lift the boys up with his teasing banter and his ability to be one of them was a gift.

He didn't say anything for a moment, just looked at her thoughtfully, and she wondered what he was thinking. "Thanks, that means a lot."

She thought for a moment he was going to say something else, but then his lip quirked up on one side and moved into a tight smile as he rose. "I guess we'd better join the group. They look like they're getting restless."

It was true, Sammy had just slipped a handful of dirt down Caleb's shirt and a dirt fight was in the making. "Yup, you definitely need to step in on that," she said, and followed him as he strode toward the "fun" breaking loose.

He'd been about to say something before duty called—and as she followed him she couldn't help wondering what it had been. There was more to Rowdy than met the eye—more than the good-time cowboy— and she was certain of that.

Not that it changed anything.

Over the next week Lucy spent time getting the house cleaned up. She had the floor people come out and look at the floors that needed replacing because she'd ripped the walls out, and they were coming back at the end of the week to lay the new floors. Thankfully the contractor had come into the house and spent one day finishing the wall openings that she'd made. Her house was coming together.

Sitting at the breakfast bar and sipping a cup of

coffee, she had her computer opened and was studying the photos she had taken of the ranch. She had a problem—she needed to find new places to paint. Her fingers were finally itching to work. It felt so right—like a long-lost friend returning.

The gloom that had hung over her past few paintings had disappeared and the sun had finally come back out for her.

Pausing on one of the photos she'd taken, she saw that she'd captured Rowdy's contagious come-play-with-me smile. The man just oozed charisma. She didn't even remember snapping the picture, but she'd been shooting rapid-fire clicks and there he was. She took a sip of her coffee and studied the photo.

Instantly, her pulse skittered. When he looked at her, Lucy couldn't explain the feelings that swept through her.

Sunshine.

Warmth, and excitement. Not to mention that she lost her train of thought and her good sense at the same time.

The small voice in the back of her mind warned that he—that men—couldn't be trusted. And yet he'd done nothing to make her think otherwise. In fact, she'd moved to the outskirts of Dew Drop and found herself immersed in a male-dominant area. Men were everywhere, and if they weren't men they were boys, teens and nearly men.

And they were all good to her.

How could she hold Tim's sins against them?

Her finger tapped rapidly on the counter beside the computer as frustration set in. She couldn't help the fear that gripped her when thinking about letting a man have the power to hurt her like that again.

Standing, she snapped off the computer and walked outside. Moose was sitting on the corner of the porch railing cleaning his paws with his tongue. He stopped and stared at her with green eyes as if assessing her.

"Hey, Moose, don't judge me," Lucy snapped, and headed out to see the progress of her studio. It had only been a week, and yet the contractor was making good time. His crew of four guys worked like ants, each with a job to do, and they were getting it done. Which was great because Margo, her agent, had been leaving messages. She had to have something new soon. The art show of the year was coming up and she needed to have something in it. True, but until now she'd not wanted to think about it.

Mac stuck his head out of the large window that they'd already installed on the side of the loft. "Hey, Lucy, got a second to come up here?"

"On my way." Taking a big breath, she headed to the studio and banished thoughts of Rowdy right out of her mind.

Walking into the barn, she stared toward the loft area that only extended out over half the ground floor. The wall was almost finished that would close it off from the downstairs except for a large window that would enable her to look out over the first floor. Hurrying up the stairs, she pushed open the door and stepped into her new studio.

"What do you think?" Mac asked. He was a large man with a jovial smile. "Give me a couple more days and she's all yours."

"Are you kidding me? It's only been a week."

"We buckled down and since I brought the men in from the other job that stalled out on us, we were able to double up on the work. You'll be painting in here next week. If that's okay with you."

"It's more than okay. I can hardly wait."

The floors were white pinewood planks they'd laid then stained and sealed. Overhead they'd left the rafters open. The focal point was the large window on the outer wall of the barn, allowing her a gorgeous view of the house and valley. It let the much-needed light stream into the room. On the back wall was a cabinet with storage for her supplies. And then there was the wall space for showcasing her work as it was being finished.

"This is fantastic." She gave the man a hug and he blushed.

"I'm going to have to see some of your work. I may want to buy my wife a present."

"I need to get crackin' and get some subject matter."

"Boy, you live near some of the prettiest country in these parts."

"I know. I've been exploring some." She told him about teaching the boys art lessons and he was impressed.

"You've got the best showing you the place. Rowdy was always exploring growing up. He spent days at a time camping all over that ranch. He knows every nook and cranny, that's for sure."

A few minutes later Lucy was in her car heading to the ranch. If Rowdy was the best to help her find the unique beauty of the ranch, then she was going to ask him to show her around some more. After all, they were neighbors, and they were just going to have to put this thing between them aside.

He was doing his part. She had to do hers and stop thinking about him all the time.

Maybe the more they got used to being around each other, the easier it would be.

Sure it would. She was ready to try, anyway. And the need to paint gave her incentive to overcome anything.

Even Rowdy.

Rowdy was mounting his horse when Lucy drove into the yard. Mixed emotions slammed into him at the same time. He was glad to see her, but at the same time seeing her sure made it hard on a guy who was trying keep her off his mind.

"Hi," she said, hopping out of her truck.

He tugged on the cinch of his horse. He knew good and well it was just fine, but it gave him something to do. Lucy wore large black shades that hid her eyes and he regretted the loss, but at the same time not seeing those eyes helped him.

"No art class or wrestling class today." He hadn't meant his words to sound negative. "What's got you out and about?"

"I need more scenes. Places that inspire me to paint. And I was wondering if I could impose on you again and ask you to show me around some more?"

He concentrated on his saddle. Patience and progress. She was torturing him.

"Sure," he said, finally looking at her. She and God were determined to make this hard on him. "I'm riding over to check on the branding and you're welcome to ride, too. There's some places not too far that I could show you. Plus, I don't know if you're into a Western branding scene, but you'll sure see one."

She tugged her shades off, exposing those killer eyes. "That sounds great. But I'm not the best rider in the world. I've done it a few times but that's it."

"Cupcake will work great for you." She was going riding with him. The idea had him smiling even if he was going to have to be on his best behavior. "I'll go saddle her up and be right back."

"I'll get my stuff together."

"Stuff?"

"My camera."

He nodded. "Oh, right. Be back in a minute."

He had Cupcake saddled and ready in a flash and led the old horse out of the stable. Lucy stared at the big horse.

"She's big."

"And easygoing. This is a beginner horse. You'll be fine. I promise."

She nodded and he wondered if she was going to trust him. When she touched Cupcake's soft neck and spoke sweetly to the horse, he knew everything would be all right. Everything but him.

Lucy had to have Rowdy help her get into the saddle. She was far too short to get her leg up in the stirrup. He lifted her effortlessly and she grabbed the saddle horn and threw her other leg over the saddle. Rowdy had to give her a little shove so she could get up there and sit straight. Otherwise she'd have been hanging off to the side.

"Thanks," she murmured once she was settled. Hanging on to the saddle horn, she tried to look more confident than she felt. It had been a very long time. He looked up at her, his hand resting on her leg.

"You sure you're okay?"

"Uh-huh," she said, seeing something deep in the depths of his eyes that touched a dark corner of her heart. It shook her. "I'm fine."

He nodded, pulled his hand away and headed to his horse. In a graceful, fluid movement he stepped into the stirrup and swung his leg over the horse's back. He settled into the saddle as though it was as comfortable to him as sitting down or standing up.

Lucy would have gone home if she could have gotten off the horse by herself. What had she been thinking? It was as if the man was irresistible to her. How could that be?

"Okay, let's go." He and his horse took off as she took her reins. She tugged on them, then clicked her tennis shoes on Cupcake's sides to try to get the horse to follow Rowdy, who was already turning the corner at the arena.

"Come on, Cupcake. Don't make me look like an idiot." When the horse didn't move, she started making clicking noises and gently urging the horse with her heels again. "Yah," she said. "Giddyap."

Rowdy rode back to her. "You haven't done this much?"

"That's what I told you," she said irritably.

"Behave, Cupcake," he scolded the horse, and gave a gentle slap to the horse's rump. Cupcake started walking. Rowdy walked his horse beside them as they slowly started moving.

Lucy could feel the sting of embarrassment on her cheeks. She was probably as red as the horse stable.

They rode across the pasture in silence and over the incline. In the distance she could see a large group of cattle and a lot of horses and cowboys. There was a group bent down, working the branding irons, but from this distance she didn't recognize any of them. She wasn't sure if they let the boys out of school for something like this or not.

"Are the boys down there?" she asked at last.

"Yeah, they love to help with the branding. Jolie works with them to get their assignments done in a situation like this. Working on the ranch is a little different. We feel it gives the boys a sense of pride to join in and these boys need all of that they can get. Some are really beat down when they get to us. Their self-esteem is in the cellar and this helps boost them up."

"I think it's great. The entire situation is so inspiring. It makes me want to paint them."

He gave her a sidelong glance. "I think that's a good thing. Speaking of, when are you going to show me some of your work?"

He seemed insistent on seeing her work; she fought the smile that nearly burst to her lips. "My studio is almost done. Mac pulled in some extra help and cut the process in half. I'll have some paintings up then. Not that I keep many hanging around. Most are in the gallery in Austin and the gallery on the River Walk in San Antonio."

"I'll see what you have and maybe when I'm near I'll stop in at one of the galleries." He smiled, and she smiled back.

"You don't have to do that."

"I know, but I want to."

She didn't know what to say and suddenly looked as if he'd said something wrong.

"Hey, Mac is a good guy. I knew he'd do a good job for you. He's spent a lot of time out here," he said, suddenly wiping away the personal direction the conversation had taken.

She realized she didn't like the wall between them but she'd asked for it. "He told me. He also said the same thing your dad did, that you were the guy to show me the ranch."

"I'm your man. When it comes to seeing the ranch," he added quickly. "I tended to spend a lot of my rebel years camping out here alone any chance I got…and sometimes when I should have been in school."

They'd almost reached where the branding was in progress and she regretted it.

"So you came out here to be alone?" she asked over the lowing of fifty or so cattle.

"Yeah, I didn't take my mom's death all that well and then I had trouble sharing the ranch, at first, with a bunch of kids I didn't know or want to know."

So he'd been angry. "Life isn't always fair, is it?"

"Nope, but you would know all about that, wouldn't you? I got nothing on you. Or these boys here."

"Lucy!"

Lucy tugged her gaze away from his and searched for who was calling out to her. She spotted little B.J. waving from where he was carrying a branding iron to the calf a couple of cowboys were holding down.

"Watch me," he shouted. And then he branded the calf.

"He looks ten feet tall," she gasped. "You're a regular cowpoke," she called to him.

His smile was wider than he was. "I got the *moooves,*" he mooed, making Lucy laugh.

"That kid blesses my soul."

Rowdy chuckled. "Yeah, he does that."

"I need to take pictures. Will I be in the way?"

"I'd rather you try to do it from the horse—unless you get the hankering to come down and help with the branding."

"I'll stay right here and, now that Cupcake has warmed up to me, I'll move around a little, too. Thanks for bringing me."

"Any time," he said, tipping his hat as he headed over to where the action was.

Reaching for her camera hanging from around her neck, she started snapping shots. She couldn't stop herself from letting the first shot be of Rowdy.

After all, he had brought her out here.

Chapter Fourteen

"I see you brought your friend," Tucker said, tugging his aviators down to let Rowdy see the questions in his McDermott-blue eyes.

Rowdy squinted through the haze at him, since the sun was over Tucker's shoulder and he hadn't worn his shades. "She's taking pictures—looking for subject matter for her artwork."

"That's why she just snapped your picture."

Rowdy's brother liked to kid. "Yeah, right."

"I'm serious. She pointed that camera straight at you as you rode off. Believe what you want, but the pretty lady got you on that camera of hers."

It was all he could do not to look over his shoulder. Or not to let the pleasure show from knowing Lucy had taken a picture of him. Maybe she wasn't as immune to him as she wanted to be. The idea gave him a shot of hope. One he knew he wanted more than anything he'd wanted in a long time.

Lucy was having a great time. She had quickly realized that cattle branding made for great photo opportunities. She had Cupcake trotting on the outskirts of the group so that she could get different angles and different facial expressions of the boys' faces as they worked. It was wonderful. One minute their faces were serious with concentration, then they were throwing their heads back and hooting with laughter at some joke someone told—usually that someone being Rowdy. The man was like a lightbulb even in the bright sunlight. He was so good with the boys.

Lucy's heart thrilled at the thought of capturing these images on canvas. It was a very welcome feeling, one she'd missed greatly.

Wes's cockiness reminded her of Rowdy. Joseph was so soft-spoken yet tenacious and Tony, the quiet one, shot her shy looks when he thought she wasn't watching him. And then there were the younger ones, so many of them so thrilled with being a working cowboy. All of the boys looked up to Morgan, Tucker and Rowdy.

They'd been working for about two hours when Rowdy pulled his hat from his head and slapped it across the front of his jeans. Dust rose about him and, just as he looked her way grinning, she snapped a shot that captured the pure essence of the man.

Her heart was thudding, and she lowered the camera, grabbed the reins and urged Cupcake to move on. She didn't need to look at Rowdy anymore—he made her stumble.

Made her stop thinking straight.

She decided it was time to head back to the barn and let Cupcake be free and, since they were all busy, she didn't bother them as she headed back toward the barn. But Cupcake had different ideas. Halfway to the crest, the goofy horse took off at a teeth-jarring trot, heading for the open range.

What was wrong?

"St-stop," Lucy chattered, bouncing on the saddle like a ball bearing on corrugated tin—through her jostling she saw bees. Cupcake, having seen them, too, or felt them, made an awful whinny noise and went from a jaw-breaking trot to a gallop.

Lucy didn't even have time to yell. Off they went toward the horizon, with Lucy leaning forward, clinging to the saddle horn. Her camera swung from around her neck, slapping the poor horse on the side and probably making matters worse by scaring the poor animal.

She didn't know much about a horse, but she knew the huge horse must have been stung by the bees—or had decided it was getting away, and quicker than Lucy wanted. Miraculously, Lucy was managing to hang on, but she didn't know how long that was going to last.

Rowdy had already taken off after Lucy when she'd started back toward the stable. He hadn't meant to stay at the branding so long, but she'd been busy taking pictures, so he had lost track of time until he'd caught her riding off. The instant Cupcake had started trotting, he'd known something was up. He knew the old horse was in distress about something. He'd urged his horse into a gallop immediately.

He'd shortened the distance, only to see Cupcake shoot to a gallop, with Lucy clinging to the saddle horn as they disappeared over the horizon.

Praying and riding hard as he topped the hill, he was not sure what he'd find on the other side. Lucy was still in the saddle.

She might be small, but she'd managed somehow not to fall off, though she'd slid so far to the right, he didn't think she'd last much longer. He finally rode up beside her and could reach out for her.

The minute his arm started round her, she turned her head. "Rowdy!" Her eyes were wide with fear.

"Let go. I've got you."

Without hesitating, she did as he asked and he swept her onto the saddle with him. She turned instantly and threw her arms around him, clinging to him as he pulled his horse to a halt.

"It's okay. I've got you," he said into her silky hair, breathing in the scent of her and feeling her heart thundering against his.

She nodded her head against his neck but didn't let up on her hold on him—and in that instant he knew he didn't want her to. He knew with all his heart that if it were up to him, he would never let her go.

Rubbing her hair gently with his hand, he just let the moment be. In the distance, Cupcake continued galloping.

"B-bees," Lucy mumbled, answering his question about what had come over the gentle horse.

"They'll do that. But you're okay now."

He half expected someone to ride up behind him, but when no one did, he knew that she'd been out of their sight range when the horse had acted up. He was glad he'd been watching and gone after her, or she very well could have been in trouble and no one would have known.

He sent up a prayer of thanks to the Man Upstairs.

Lifting her head, she gave a shaky smile. "Thanks,

cowboy." Her voice was as shaky as her smile. "I thought I was done for—or heading to the border."

He chuckled. "You've got skills, Lucy Calvert. You held on longer than I expected. Might be some Calamity Jane in you after all."

"Ha, only by the grace of God."

"True. But I didn't want to say so."

They laughed and it felt as if they were the only two people in the world. Rowdy had to do everything in his power not to kiss her—or even appear as though he was thinking about it. But, boy, was he.

He cared for Lucy. More than he'd ever cared for a woman. And he wasn't sure what he was going to do about it. When she found out what he'd done…she wouldn't have anything to do with him. She'd never, ever trust him.

His heart started thundering.

Lucy's gaze feathered over his face like a caress— she probably wasn't even aware how she was looking at him or what it was doing to him. When her eyes stopped on his lips he bit back a need to crush her to him and kiss her, to feel the softness of her lips against his. He halted his thinking.

He had to be honorable.

If he wanted even the most remote shot at a future with Lucy—and he did—then he had to step carefully and move slowly. He could not mess up again. Lucy had to trust him before he ever thought about kissing her again.

Then tell her about what you did!

"I'd better get you home," he said. He couldn't tell her. Not now, not until the time was right.

When is the time going to be right?

His horse stirred beneath them, reminding him they weren't moving. There was a creek not too far away and he saw Cupcake halt on the bank and begin drinking water.

Wrapping an arm around Lucy, he held her lightly as he urged his horse forward. The sky was darkening ahead of them, but he figured the rain would hold off for a couple of hours.

"Where are we going?" Lucy shifted and studied the pasture ahead of them.

"To that line of trees up ahead. There's a stream there. I thought you might want to see it."

She nodded, but didn't say anything. Within minutes they were there.

"Oh," she gasped. "This is beautiful."

He pointed. "When the setting sun is filtering through those trees, it takes on a golden hue."

As if on cue, the dark clouds parted and the sun broke free for a few seconds. Light streaked through the trees and the creek came alive with a lively glow.

Automatically his arm tightened around Lucy's waist.

She turned to look at him and he knew it was time to get off the horse.

It was either that or he was going to kiss her, no doubt about it.

Weak-kneed when her feet touched the ground, Lucy tried not to wobble as she headed toward the water's edge, putting distance between her and Rowdy. The knowledge that she trusted him swept over her like the warm glow that had just burst through the dark clouds.

That trust changed everything about her since waking up in that burn center, alone, scared and scarred.

When her heart had been closed up tightly, she hadn't thought much about her body. She'd just been grateful to be alive and that her face and hands had been spared. But now, in an instant of discovery and recovery she'd become aware... What would a man—Rowdy—think of her scarred body?

What would a husband think of the sight of her?

The thought was almost more than she could bear. She wrapped her arms about her waist and prayed for the images to fade away from her mind. For God to give her answers.

She felt exhausted and emotionally drained as Rowdy came up behind her and gently tugged at her hair.

"Penny for your thoughts," he said.

She closed her eyes, but couldn't trust herself to speak.

Rowdy walked down the creek, putting distance between them. He seemed restless—bothered. After a minute he swung back around. "I have to say something."

His tone startled her. "Okay."

"I, um... Look, there is no easy way to say this. I rushed kissing you before because that's what I do. That's what I've always done. If I see something I like, or want, I go for it. No waiting patiently for me. I just go for it. And where women are concerned, that's always been the way I operated." He paused, looking uncomfortable as he tugged at his collar.

She knew he had a wild background. But hearing him talk about his...love life brought the wall back up around her heart. She hadn't even realized it had just fallen down.

"Lucy, I'm changed."

Anger that she'd let her guard down crushed over her. "You kissed me the other day out of the blue. How is that 'changed'?" The memory of the kiss surged through her as if it had been only a few seconds since he'd planted his lips on hers.

His eyes filled with distress. "I know. But—I honestly went a little crazy when we were fighting over that sledgehammer. And I didn't know your story then. I've tried to prove that to you since you shared your story with me."

She hugged herself tighter. Locking her heart down tight. "Yes. I see that. But—"

He came to stand in front of her. The gurgling stream's soothing song only played the tension that was suddenly between them. How could she have even thought she could trust a man who had been with so many women?

"I'm trying to change. I have changed. I haven't dated…for about a year. I'm working at not just jumping in—I've committed to the Lord not to be that man anymore."

But how could she trust that this was true? Lucy's mind filled with the deceit that Tim had pulled off and she'd never even suspected.

Staring at Rowdy, she didn't think this could get any worse. But she was wrong….

"You need to know the rest of my story, too," he said, glancing at his boots before meeting her eyes. "I got in trouble about ten months ago when I got mixed up with a married woman—"

Lucy gasped. "A married woman."

"I didn't know."

"How could you not know?" Contempt rang in her words at his excuse. Lucy couldn't believe what he was saying.

"I didn't know her well enough before I— Well, you know. Before I got involved."

Completely disgusted, she spun toward Cupcake. She wanted out of here. Away from him, and if that meant getting back on that horse then so be it. She'd walk away if she had to she was so mad at him.

"Lucy, I'm changed. I am."

She glared over her shoulder at him. "Ha! You kissed me before."

"Yeah, I know. But—"

"Nope, can't do it." Cupcake looked up from where she'd moved and was now eating grass, but didn't spook as Lucy took the reins in her hand. She stretched to reach up and grab the saddle horn, but Cupcake was too tall for her to do it on her own.

"Hey," Rowdy snapped, coming to stand beside her. "I'm trying to talk to you. To tell you that I'm trying to change. That I'm working at not just jumping in—"

Lucy swung around and jammed a finger in his chest. "Do you even have any compassion for the spouse? For what you put him through?"

"Yeah, even after he busted my nose I felt bad for the guy. But that didn't change anything. And until he showed up, I was clueless."

"Yeah, well, clueless hits both parties and it's not a good feeling."

"Look, I know I'm a jerk. I'm sorry it happened to you but I don't date married women."

"How do you know? If you didn't even take the time to get to know your, your lady friends, then how do you know this was the only one? And besides, I'm sure that excuse made the husband feel okay about the whole incident." She felt tears leak from the edge of her eyes and brushed them away. He looked defeated suddenly and she hardened her heart as he raked his hands through his hair.

"You have a point," he said quietly. "I'll help you up and take you home."

She nodded in agreement, so ready to be gone. Swiping at her face with her fingertips, she turned toward the horse and let Rowdy lift her up so that she could get her foot in the stirrup.

"I can make it back on my own," she said, and turning Cupcake around, they were off at a slow pace. No bees were in sight.

It wouldn't have mattered anyway. She was so numb she wouldn't have felt them even if they'd swarmed her.

Rowdy just stood there and watched Lucy ride away.

Telling her the truth had been a really bad idea. Worst idea of the decade—aside from his involvement with Liz.

He'd known he was doomed the moment the confession came out of his mouth. But regardless of the churning in his gut, he'd known that he had to come clean. And despite the look of accusation that had crept into Lucy's eyes, he'd forced himself to be honest even as he realized it was going to cost him all of Lucy's respect.

It hit him that she probably felt as foolish as he

had when she'd learned that her husband hadn't been faithful.

Her tears glistening on her long, dark lashes had finished him off, making him feel every bit the dirtbag that he was.

Lucy was better off without him. As she disappeared over the ridge, he knew she deserved so much more than him.

Truth was, if they hadn't had this conversation—or attempted to have this conversation—he might have continued to let himself believe that she could actually have been the one he was waiting on.

Suddenly bone weary, Rowdy walked over and stared at the creek. And he started praying.

Chapter Fifteen

Rowdy McDermott was a womanizer just like Tim had been.

Men could not be trusted.

Oh, they were fine if you just didn't get personal with them. And she'd already gotten far too personal with Rowdy. She'd planned all along to keep him at arm's length, but the man had forced himself into this new life. That was the thing that really had her angry.

It wasn't as if she'd asked him to come around.

No, he'd manipulated her. Toyed with her.

Her worst mistakes seemed destined to repeat themselves on an endless loop.

She was thankful that the ranch appeared deserted when she got back to the barn. Walter Pepper called, "Hello," from the end of the barn when she rode in. Thankfully he seemed busy with a horse. He told her to just tie Cupcake to the stall and he'd take care of her.

Since Lucy had no idea what to do to take care of the horse anyway, she gladly agreed and ran to her truck. She couldn't get home soon enough.

Painting was the answer—she needed to work,

needed the release painting had always been for her up until the aftermath of Tim's betrayal and the fire had stolen it from her. Thank goodness the studio was almost done. Thank goodness she had a renewed passion for the work and the release it offered her.

Whether she was painting anything saleable didn't matter—she was as mad as she'd ever been.

Where had all these problems come from? She'd arrived here with one goal—to get rid of the anger eating up inside. The wall destruction had helped, or so she'd thought. But she knew now that it had only been a temporary fix. The anger was like a living thing eating away inside of her. Hearing Rowdy confess that he, too, was a womanizing fool had relit that fire to a blazing inferno.

Men!

Of course, she knew infidelity wasn't completely limited to men. Women had the same dysfunction. Her mother had proved that—over and over.

Her dad had moved on. He was extremely happy with his new wife and Lucy was happy for him. He deserved to be happy. Still, what her mother had put them through had ended Lucy's childhood.

She was so thankful she and Tim hadn't had children.

At least there was that.

Pulling her paint box from the storage box, she saw the picture album beneath it.

Lucy hadn't realized she'd packed it. She just stared at it in the bottom of the box. Her fingers trembled as she lifted it out. She knew what was inside. Pictures of the lie she'd lived.

If the burn pile had been going, she'd have walked straight out the door and tossed the album in the fire.

Instead, she sat it against the wall. She was moving forward, not back. And pictures of her and Tim had no place in her future. Whatever good times they'd had were wiped away the day his "female friend" had walked into her room at the burn center and spilled her story.

Funny, Lucy thought it was supposed to be the victim who took revenge. But it had been the opposite way in her story.

Of course in Rowdy's story, it was as it should be. The spouse got the lick in—or she should say the fist.

Good for that guy.

"What's gotten into you?" his dad asked a few days after he and Lucy had had their fight. They were separating calves out to take to the cattle sale and his dad had decided that today would be a good day to get out of the office. Rowdy had a feeling it was to look over his shoulder. His next statement proved him right.

"You've been hard to live with and work with the past few days, so the men have said. What's bothering you?"

Yeah, he was ornery. That was for certain.

Why had he agreed to help Lucy milk a wild heifer?

After they'd parted ways, she'd shown back up for practice because the rodeo was coming up and she was determined to keep her end of the bargain.

"The stubborn woman wants to milk the wild heifer. And I'm afraid she's going to get hurt."

Randolph moved with his horse as it danced to stop

a calf from escaping back to the group of cattle they'd just taken it from.

"You'll take care of her. The guys will control the calf."

Rowdy scowled and his dad laughed.

"You and I both know those cows we put in there aren't range heifers. They are going to be more scared than wild. Wes, Tony and Joseph will have no trouble."

Rowdy stared out across the pasture. His dad was right, but he still didn't like it.

"How deep are you in?"

At his dad's question, Rowdy met his gaze. There was concern etched in the creases around his eyes.

"Deep." There was no use denying what he knew his dad could see. He was in love with Lucy Calvert.

A smile flashed across Randolph's face. "Lucy's a good match for you. Your mother would be pleased."

His heart tightened as he thought about his mother— of all the years he'd longed to make her proud of him. He took a deep breath and held his father's gaze. "It's not that simple. Let's get these in the pen and then I'll tell you about it."

They worked with Chet, their top hand, and the other ranch hands getting the calves into the holding pen. When they were done, Rowdy and his dad loaded their horses up in the trailer and then rode back in the truck together.

"So what's really got you twisted in knots?"

Rowdy raked his hand through his hair and let out a breath before confiding Lucy's background. It wasn't his story to tell, but his father was a man of great integrity.

"You're not going to just walk away from this?" Randolph asked when he was done.

"I don't want to, but Lucy has already been through enough. She doesn't need me and my messed-up background reminding her of what her no-good husband did to her. The man took away her ability to trust. If she stays like she is, she could end up alone for the rest of her life."

"*I'm* alone and managing fine. But I'm twentysomething years older than she is, I figure. So I'd hate to see that happen. Are you going to let it happen?"

"What can I do?"

"You can help her learn to trust again. You can start by being there for her."

"She's barely speaking to me now."

"Then what do you have to lose? If you're serious about this new walk with the Lord, then you have to do this because of the man you've become. Not the man you were. You made a mistake. The difference is you've changed and are holding yourself accountable for your actions now. That's all you can do other than keep proving yourself trustworthy."

"You're sure you're ready for this tomorrow night?" Nana asked Lucy. They were in the Spotted Cow Café or, as the men and the boys liked to call it, the Cow Patty Café because of the painted brown spots gone wrong on the concrete floor.

Lucy stared at a dancing-cow figurine sitting on the table. It was one of an abundant cow paraphernalia collection that practically hid the walls of the café, there were so many. "I think so. All I have to do is get a drop of milk. The fellas are going to take care of the cow."

"Yeah, but who is gonna take care of you?" Edwina slapped a hand to her hip. "I've seen those cow-milking contests. Grown men fall underneath the animal thinking for some reason it might be easier to milk the cow lying on their back while getting stomped on." She shook her head. "No, sister, this is not a good idea. And to think I took you for an intelligent sort the first time I saw you."

Lucy chuckled. "Edwina, I am not going to get stomped on. Rowdy told me not to go for the bag until he gives me the go-ahead. So rest easy, I'm not getting thrown under the cow."

Edwina made a face that clearly said she didn't believe it, and then left to take an order from a herd of cowboys on the far side of the café.

Ms. Jo had come out of the kitchen and heard the last half of the conversation. "Ed get you straightened out?" she asked, sliding into the booth beside Nana.

"No, but she gave it a good try," Lucy said.

The diner door was yanked opened and Mabel came hustling inside. "The Dew Drop Inn's been busier than an ant colony today," she declared, squeezing her large-framed body into the booth seat beside Lucy.

"With all these ranch-rodeo teams arriving, this should be a good weekend for the town."

"Café's been swamped, too." Ms. Jo fanned herself. "The pie baking's been going nonstop."

Jolie came over from the jukebox just as Blake Shelton started singing "Austin." "I love this song. It's an old one but just makes me think of happy endings," she said.

Mabel had taken Jolie's spot, so she pulled up a chair.

"Speaking of happy endings." Mabel turned her full attention toward Lucy. Now, Mabel was a good size bigger than Lucy, and she'd effectively trapped Lucy in the booth. There was nowhere to go.

"Look, I know y'all are all hoping that something happens between Rowdy and me, but it's not going to."

Ms. Jo's eyebrows squeezed together and a V formed above her glasses. "You cannot tell us you don't like that good-looking cowboy."

Everyone started talking at once about how right they were for each other. After they'd all quieted down, she told them her story. She couldn't believe she'd held it in so long.

"Of all the horrible things." Mabel's voice was gentle as she threw an arm around Lucy and gave her a hug. "That brings back memories."

"Tell her, Mabel," Jolie said, and everyone echoed her.

Ms. Jo gave Mabel a nod. "If anyone knows how you feel, it's Mabel. She didn't have a fire, but she got a raw deal."

Lucy was curious now. She knew that Mabel had never been married.

"I was in love once, a long time ago. Paul was a handsome cowboy with a smile that could turn girls' insides to jelly. I knew better than to be foolish enough to fall for the man, but sometimes a heart will do what a heart wants to do and there's nothing you can do about it."

"Tell me about it," Edwina said as she passed by. "I've done fell for three men and not a winner in the bunch." Shaking her head, she kept right on moving toward the kitchen with a new order.

"On this I have to agree with Ed. Paul took my heart and then he decided mine wasn't enough and so he took a few more on the side. Deception is a tough thing to overcome." Her usual jovial good humor was gone. "After I discovered what he'd been doing, I gave him 'what for' every which way I could. That poor man thought his life was in danger. It *was*. But I decided breaking him into pieces wasn't going to help ease my pain any, so I watched him ride away. And I can tell you losing the desire to trust another man like that is a shame."

Lucy wrapped her hand around Mabel's and gave a supportive squeeze. Mabel slipped her hand out and covered Lucy's and continued talking. "There are times when I do regret that I let him take that away from me."

Jolie looked sad; her beautiful green eyes misted. "I almost did that to Morgan, and it is the regret of my life that I hurt him when I chose my career over him and left. God had a plan for us, but if I hadn't come back, there was a very good possibility he might never have married."

Lucy was shocked by both stories. She wasn't sure what to say. "I'm glad it worked out for you and Morgan, Jolie. Mabel, what happened to Paul? Did you ever see him again?"

She tucked her hair behind her ear and shook her head. "Never did. Never wanted to. I've been happy for the most part. I have my mission trips that I'm called to do and I have my Dew Drop Inn and believe me, folks do drop in." Her eyes sparkled. "That place keeps me busy. God's been very good to me. And to be honest, I have no problem with men in general. There are men in this town whom I trust with all my heart. Those McDermott men are four of them. Don't mean I want to fall in love with any of them, though. There's not anyone I want to fall in love with—I'm too old now anyway. But I'm telling you, girl, you need to think long and hard about letting your heart harden up like you're doing."

"You know, that's right," Nana said at last. "Rowdy is my grandson and I love that boy dearly. And I'm not making excuses for him, but he took his momma's death hard. He has a lot to offer a woman and I think the woman who wins his heart is going to be a very blessed woman."

Lucy suddenly felt as though she was being ganged up on. And she wasn't sure what to think about that. It wasn't as if they were trying to fix her up. They just all thought so much of Rowdy that she felt the pressure tenfold to decide that she was wrong.

"It's something I don't know if I can do. Honestly, I do have feelings for him. I think that's why I'm so mad at him."

At her words all eyes lit up like Christmas lights.

"Hold on. I'm just saying that's why this is so hard. Because he's very lovable. And I am not saying I'm in love. I'm saying— Oh, I don't know what I'm saying! I'm about as confused as a woman can be."

Mabel patted her hand. "There, there. We'll just pray that God's will be done. You just try to keep an open heart."

All the way home, Lucy thought about that. How could she keep an open heart when she was terrified of doing exactly that?

She hadn't told them the truth, either. The whole story. Just like she hadn't told Rowdy. Ever since she'd begun to have these conflicting emotions concerning him, she'd found herself lingering in front of the mirror and staring at the burns that covered her body. It was more than she could ask of any man.

She could barely look at them herself.

Chapter Sixteen

The night of the wild-cow milking had arrived. She'd practiced two more times since she and Rowdy had fought and they'd made it through the practice by communicating with the kids more than each other. It had been awkward for both of them.

But tonight it would be over, and there were just a couple more weeks of art class and after that, they could steer clear of each other.

Was that what she wanted?

One minute. And then the next, no.

All she knew for certain was that tonight she was going to milk a wild cow and not get herself killed. That was her agenda.

The stands were full when she, Wes, Joseph, Tony and Rowdy joined the other wild-cow milkers.

"Go Sunrise Ranch Team!" came yells from the stands, from boys who were screaming at the top of their lungs. Everyone in the group turned to search the stands. Not hard to find, the other thirteen Sunrise Ranch kids stood in the middle, waving and jumping with excitement. Sammy and B.J. held a sign with the word Go painted above a yellow sunrise.

Behind them sat Nana, Mabel, Ms. Jo, Morgan and Jolie.

Tucker, on duty, had wished them luck as they'd passed him on their way into the pens. And Randolph was standing on the other side of the gate at the opening of the arena with some of the ranch hands. She wondered if they were there in case they were needed. That worried her, despite knowing the paramedics were there.

"Y'all've got a cheering section," Rowdy said from where he sat on his horse.

Tony's half grin hitched upward. "All the ranch hands are hanging on to the railing down there, too, with Mr. Randolph. You know they're going to be yelling when it's our turn."

"I'm glad we drew first," Joseph said. "I'd be nervous if we had to wait until the end."

"Me, too," Lucy finally added. She'd been trying to calm the butterflies in her stomach but had finally given up. She was nervous and there wasn't anything that could be done about it.

She met Rowdy's smile with a weak one of her own.

"You'll be fine. Just remember to let us get the cow stopped and then I'll give you the okay to dash in and get the milk."

"She's got it in the bag," Wes said, his confidence sounding far higher than anything Lucy remotely felt.

The PA broadcast the start of the wild-cow milking and Lucy froze. Then to her dismay, the gate opened and they entered the arena. Well, they did, but she almost didn't follow until she forced her feet to move.

From inside the arena, the grandstands looked huge. The boys were grinning and waving at the crowd as if they'd already won. Wes became a clown. His eyes danced as he whipped his hat from his head and waved it at the crowd. He pumped his hands up and down to get the crowd to roar—it was as if he were born for this. Joseph and Tony just grinned beside him. They were all too cute.

Rowdy looked especially nice tonight in his red shirt, black hat and signature grin. She wished he'd stop flashing that distracting grin around! Of course, him sitting like a champion himself on one of his champion horses, looking ready to shine as he did, was distracting, too. And not just to her. Lucy had no doubt that every female in the stands had absolutely no idea there were three kids and a lady in the arena with him.

He turned his horse and trotted back to her side. "How are you doing?"

That he'd thought of her put a catch in her heart and, looking up at him, she suddenly felt breathless and young and free…as if none of the heavy burdens of her past was hanging over her. "I'm good, thanks for asking."

He leaned down in the saddle, his expression intent. "Good. Now, I'm compelled to remind you—do not get within reach of that heifer's legs until I'm in position between you and her back leg. Is that clear?"

He was worried about her. She nodded. "Clear."

Sitting up, he looked satisfied with her answer. She couldn't grasp what she felt but…watching him, her heart felt full.

Wes turned to her—leaving his adoring fans for a moment and making Lucy smile. "The dude down there on the end standing inside that white circle of lime is who you race to with the milk."

She nodded. After she got at least a drop of milk into the small jar in her hand, she had to run to the man in the circle. The hard work of the team didn't count if she failed in her task. She prayed that she didn't fall down and spill the milk. The boys had done their part painting their pictures; now she had to do her part.

Joseph grinned at her. "Don't be all worried. You're going to do us proud."

"That's right," Tony added, coming to stand beside her. "You look as nervous as me."

She wanted to give him a hug but it would probably have embarrassed him. "Let's do this," she said instead, winking at him. He responded with that grin that had her heart turning over for the kid who'd been so mistreated by the parents who were supposed to love and protect him.

The announcer introduced them as the Sunrise Ranch team, then called out each of their names, and they stepped forward and waved. When their heifer entered the arena, people went wild. A lump lodged in Lucy's throat as the heifer stared at them—clearly wary. Rowdy pulled his rope from the saddle horn and readied it. When the clock started, he rode out toward the animal and the kids followed him into the center of the arena. He twirled the rope above his head, then sent the loop flying. It landed with ease over the heifer's head. Rowdy wrapped the rope around the saddle horn and his horse stepped back as the cow tried to run, but the rope pulled taut and the boys were already on the run. She went right behind them.

The cow dodged one way, but the boys moved with

it, anticipating where it would go. Lucy would have gone the opposite direction! Wes dived right in, fearless as he grabbed the cow by the neck and locked his arm around it like she'd been taught on the small calf that day. Joseph grabbed the cow's tail and dug his boots into the ground. Tony moved to help Wes. With the cow sort of under control, Rowdy came off the horse and headed toward the flank. Lucy's adrenaline was revved up and she prayed she could get the milk.

The boys grinned at her, even Wes, though he was gritting his teeth with the effort he was using to keep hold of the animal. Rowdy motioned for her to take her turn. She raced in, or at least she thought she raced in, but the cow chose that moment to try to throw its head up and drag the guys. Wes and Tony held on, Rowdy pushed the animal and Joseph leaned back so far that his seat was also dragging in the dirt as his heels bit into the ground. Lucy looked from Wes to Joseph, not sure what to do, but they got the animal almost still again. Rowdy gave her the nod again as he planted his back against the leg that could potentially lash out and nail her.

Lucy gritted her teeth and dived. She was going to get the milk this time. Holding her hand like she'd been taught, she made contact, and even when the heifer moved back she held on. She pushed, then squeezed. The animal moved. Lucy went down in the dirt but kept milking. From her prone position looking up, she saw a trickle make it into the glass jar.

"I got it," she yelled, excitement overwhelming her. Rowdy was laughing when he reached down and hauled her off the ground and set her on her feet.

"Run, Lucy, run," he said, and she did.

It seemed like miles to the man in the circle, and halfway there she saw the people in the stands in front of her stand up. She made it to the man, winded but with milk in the jar. They'd done it. She spun around but her heart stalled when she saw the heifer run over Tony, trampling him in the dirt.

Cows and steers running over people was a common occurrence in any rodeo; it was part of it. But Lucy hadn't gotten used to it and her stomach dropped and she started running.

Tony didn't jump up and grin. Rowdy was beside him by the time she made it, and the other boys had gathered around. Tony's shirt was ripped wide-open in the back. And to her relief he sat up just as she reached them. She was breathing so hard she thought she might pass out right there in the arena. He grinned at Rowdy.

"Take it easy. Your arm's not looking so good," Rowdy said, seeing a deep gash that was bleeding. Rowdy touched a bruised spot on Tony's lower back, and when he touched it, the boy flinched. But it wasn't the bruise that had Lucy's attention, it was the scars that riddled Tony's body.

Lucy's stomach lurched and it was all she could do not to lose its contents in the dirt right there in front of everyone. Dear Lord, Tony had told her he had scars, but not like this. She hadn't imagined they would be like this.

Hadn't imagined they would be worse than hers.

Her gaze met Rowdy's and he seemed to read everything in her face, because he said, "Hold on." Tony thought he was talking to him and nodded, but Lucy knew he was talking to her. She nodded, too, and couldn't stop nodding. It became compulsive and she had to will her head to stop before the boys realized how shaken she was.

"We're going to take you to the hospital and have this bruise checked out. I don't want you having an internal problem and us not knowing it."

"Aw, it's okay," Tony said, wincing as Rowdy helped him to his feet. The crowd cheered as Rowdy and Wes helped him out of the arena. The on-site doctor met them at the gate along with Randolph. They had Tony sit down. The paramedic looked him over and agreed with Rowdy that X-rays made sense as a cautionary measure.

"You did it, Lucy," Tony said, grinning up at her from his bench. The kid was tough. Her throat ached with the need to cry.

"I did," she said instead, forcing her voice to hold steady. "But it was because of you fellas. That cow didn't stand a chance."

"Let's get him to the hospital," Randolph said, and they headed out of the gate. Lucy followed close behind.

Morgan and Jolie met them at the waiting room of the small hospital in Dew Drop. Nana and Tucker had stayed back with the ranch kids at the rodeo. It was agreed that the hospital didn't need fifteen rambunctious kids swarming the small waiting room.

They were right, the hospital was very small, but then Dew Drop wasn't a metropolis and they were lucky to have the place.

Randolph, Morgan and Rowdy all went into the emergency room with Tony. Jolie and Lucy sat together and waited.

Jolie watched them disappear through the door.

"There is one thing these boys know when they come to Sunrise Ranch—they are loved."

Lucy nodded. She was still shaken about what she'd seen and ashamed that she hadn't realized when she was talking to Tony how badly he'd been injured. "What happened to Tony? I mean, with those burns. He talked to me about them, but I had no idea they were that bad. I talked to Rowdy, who said Tony's parents were responsible, but I didn't realize..." Her voice trailed off.

"I'm sorry." There was compassion in Jolie's voice and she leaned forward. "He had been burned with cigarettes for years and no one noticed. It's horrible to think that. But when his parents tossed gas on him and then a match when he was ten, he was taken away from them. From what I've been told, he had second- and third-degree burns and it took numerous skin grafts. I'm sure with your arm and neck that you understand the pain he went through."

The air had gone out of the room as Jolie spoke. Lucy felt small suddenly. Fury and anguish welled inside of her for what Tony had endured. "How," she rasped, looking down at her hands clenched in her lap, "could parents do such a thing?"

Jolie clasped her hands with her own. "It's a wicked world we live in. I can't understand, either. But Tony is alive and well and loved. And though it's been tough, what he went through, he's been on the ranch from the day he left the hospital almost four years ago. And that has been a blessing. I cried when I read his background, but I've watched him for months now, and he's one of the most well-adjusted kids considering what he's been through. Though, just like you, he doesn't like to show his scars."

Lucy sighed. "We talked about that. It's easier not to let people see them. Easier not to have to answer questions. Or to see pity on their faces."

"That's what Tony has said."

Rowdy and Morgan came out of the room and walked over to where they were. Both Jolie and Lucy stood the minute they saw them.

"What did they say?" Jolie asked.

"He has a deep bruise, but his organs are all fine, so that's a blessing. Dad's with him finishing up and they'll release him in a few minutes."

Jolie hugged Morgan. "Wonderful!"

Rowdy placed his arm across Lucy's shoulders and gave her a gentle hug. "You okay?"

She was grateful for his touch. "Yes, I'm relieved and happy that Tony wasn't hurt seriously. But I really need to talk to you about something."

"Sure." Concern etched his face. "We'll head out if y'all have it under control from here," he said to his family.

"We do," Morgan said, a rock if there ever was one. "You did good out there tonight, Lucy. I hope this accident didn't shake you up too bad. We try to protect the boys as best we can, but the truth is kids could find a way to fall off the porch and get hurt."

"I know. I get it. Y'all do a great job with the boys."

"Some folks don't understand. But we don't allow them on bulls. Dad draws the line there, so even living the cowboy way has limits at Sunrise Ranch. Much to Wes's dismay."

She'd figured out by small things he'd said that Wes wanted to ride bulls.

She went in and gave Tony a hug, a really gentle but long one, and then left, telling him she would see him back at the ranch. She and Rowdy walked out to the parking lot and he held the door of his truck for her and placed his hand at her elbow as she hoisted herself into the tall truck. Sometimes being short just got old. And then she had to admit that sometimes it had its advantages. His hand on her elbow was one of those times.

After he drove them from the parking lot, he swung through a drive-through and bought them both something to drink. Lucy hadn't even realized how much she needed the sugar in the soda until it hit her system.

He looked at her with kindness in his eyes. "Better? You were wilting on me."

His concern did funny things to her heart.

"Thanks, I did need this. Is there somewhere private we can talk?"

"Sure." He drove out of town and headed toward the ranch and her house. But he continued on past the turn and Lucy watched the scenery go by. She tried to calm the nerves trying to talk her out of what she knew she had to do.

After a while he turned and went through an entrance with the Sunrise Ranch brand.

"This is another entrance to the ranch. It's connected to the original ranch, but would be a long ride as the crow flies on horseback. We usually drive over with horses then unload when we're working cattle." She felt as though his explanation was meant more to fill the dead space floating between them than to inform her of where they were.

The moon shimmered on the white rock road and bathed the countryside with a pale glow.

He stopped beside a pond with the moon reflecting off the water. A huge tree hung out over the water, and there was a narrow pier.

"See the owl, there, sitting in the tree?" He pointed and, sure enough, Lucy saw the owl watching them, his eyes glowing yellow in the headlights.

"You spotted him quickly."

"Out here, you just have to keep your eyes open. This place is alive with animals. But that guy right there has been hunting out of that tree for years."

She smiled at him despite her nerves. She took another sip of her soda. Rowdy rolled down the windows and turned off the engine. Leaning his back against the door, he studied her.

"What did you want to talk about?"

She looked away, toward the water. "I hadn't realized how extensive Tony's burns were."

"I didn't understand that. After we talked…"

"I know you assumed Tony had told me. But he didn't show me. I could not have imagined the extent even if I'd tried."

"I'm sorry. That was why you looked so pale out there."

She nodded. He gripped the steering wheel with one hand and his knuckles grew white in the darkness. "When I saw your burns, I thought of Tony. He feels a bond with you because you have that in common."

Lucy sat her soda in the cup holder and rolled a strand of hair with her fingers, thinking about where to begin.

"I haven't been completely honest with you."

He looked startled. "That's okay."

She shook her head. "No. It's not. I've been hard on you and—" There seemed to be no air in the truck and yet the windows were open. "My burns aren't just on my arms and neck as I've let everyone think. Seeing Tony tonight hit me hard." Her voice cracked and she had to pause to get it back under control. "You see, until now, I've told myself I was okay, blessed that my face had been spared—and I am. I think that's why this is especially hard for me to admit that I'm so ashamed of my body that I haven't told anyone that the burns on my arms extend over most of my torso…" She couldn't say more.

His eyes shadowed and in the moonlight they glistened, and she could almost believe tears were there in their depths. She took a deep breath, torn by whether he was repulsed by what she was telling him or feeling compassion. Her heart of hearts said compassion, but she was uncertain how even that made her feel.

Her throat felt raw.

He looked away and studied the pond; his Adam's apple bobbed. "You—" he started and then stopped. "I can't stand the thought of you suffering like that."

"I didn't suffer long. I was knocked unconscious soon after the ceiling caved in. The recovery was… difficult. So bad I wished at times I hadn't lived."

Rowdy got out of the truck instantly and was at her door within seconds. Without ceremony he yanked it open and pulled her into his arms, crushing her to him.

"I know you'd rather I not touch you—" his voice was muffled in her hair "—but I can't stand the thought of you in so much pain."

He was holding her tightly, her toes barely brushing the ground, and Lucy's arms had somehow locked around his shoulders. She trembled as tears that had long ago dried up tried to break free at his heartfelt words and the earnest way he held her.

The owl's woeful hoot sounded, cutting through the silence. Lucy pulled herself together, very aware of the man embracing her.

He inhaled deeply and then lowered her to the ground and stepped back. Almost as if he had willed himself to do it. Lucy's heart was thundering and, though she wished with all her might that things could be different and that his arms were meant to hold her, she couldn't let herself go there.

"I didn't mean to get personal." He looked almost bashful. "But I didn't kiss you."

She laughed despite the mood over the moment. "You did very well. I needed a hug in the worst way. Thank you."

"You're welcome, anytime. Why did you share that with me?"

His question surprised her. She walked over to the pier, tested it with her foot then walked a few feet onto it. Staring down into the water, she found the moon looking back at her. Rowdy followed her, waiting at the end with a hand on each railing of the narrow pier.

"I'm not sure, really." She turned and leaned against the railing, crossing her arms. "I just saw Tony's scars and suddenly I didn't feel authentic. And I knew that in order to feel like I wasn't being dishonest that I had to be open about my burns."

"It's no one's business."

"True. But, still, I felt like I needed to tell some-one…that I needed to tell you."

Lucy wasn't sure why she'd wanted him to know. But suddenly she was afraid. Had she told too much? Had she shown him too much of her heart?

Chapter Seventeen

It was all Rowdy could do not to blurt out that he loved her. He'd had to hold her when she'd looked so shattered telling him about her burns. He'd known for certain in that instant that what he'd been thinking was true. He'd fallen in love with this beautiful woman and the reality was she would never be able to love him.

Sure, she'd confided in him. That gave him hope, but he knew deep inside that she'd never be able to give her heart to him.

"I'm ashamed of the burns," she whispered, blinking. She held his gaze for a second, and then with a shuddering breath looked away. "I worry—"

"One day you'll fall in love, Lucy. You'll find a man you can love." It wouldn't be him, but someone she could believe in. Someone honorable, and upstanding. "And when you do, your scars won't matter to him. If that's what you're worried about."

They don't matter to me.

She looked lost to him standing there.

"I think I'm ready to call it a night," she said, walking to where he stood. "Thank you for listening."

He followed her to his truck and helped her up into the cab. "Thanks for listening to me," she said again. "I just needed to talk."

"Anytime." What else could he say? He asked himself that all the way back around to his side of the truck. There was a ton of stuff he wanted to say, but nothing he could.

Silence filled the truck as he drove back toward home. "You did good out there, by the way," he finally said.

"You're a good teacher. Not that I'm planning on making a habit of it. That was most likely my last rodeo competition."

He grinned. "Quit while you're on top."

She laughed. "Something like that, anyway."

It felt good to hear her laugh. She amazed him.

When he pulled into her driveway, Moose was sitting on the cab of her truck, watching them.

"No, don't get out," she said when he started to open his door. "I'm fine. Thanks. I fell apart a little, but I feel much better now."

"Lucy, thanks for trusting me with your story. It meant a lot to me that you did that."

She paused before closing the door. "Rowdy, you've been nothing but good to me. I'm so sorry if I've been unfair to you. You said you didn't know that woman was married and I believe you. I admire that you've changed your life."

He watched her go, wanting to go after her. Bowing his head, he prayed that God would help Lucy with the struggles she was trying to face alone.

"You should ask her out."

Rowdy looked over the top of the horse he was brushing down and looked at Wes.

"Seriously, dude. We—" he pointed from himself to Joseph and the fourteen other culprits gathered around "—know you're interested in Lucy. It's plain to see."

"That's right, Rowdy." B.J. stared up at him. "We like Lucy. She done helped me paint a rock and everything. I like her and I know you got to, 'cause you ain't stupid."

Rowdy's jaw dropped and he looked at the older boys, wondering who was responsible for B.J.'s word choice.

Wes fessed up. "Hey, you're not stupid and we all know it."

"We also see you looking all funny when you look at her," Sammy added. "Ain't that right, Caleb?"

Caleb nodded his blond head. "We've seen you do it."

"Yeah," B.J. spoke up again. "It's kinda like you ain't slept in days and days. Your eyelids get droopy."

"Okay, who has been talking to this kid?"

B.J.'s brows scrunched up. "I got eyes, Rowdy. I'm almost nine years old. I know about things."

Wes and Joseph were almost hunched over holding in their laughter on the other side of the horse. Rowdy planned on having a man-to-man talk with them later.

"Look, Rowdy." Tony stepped out of the group, his face a work of concern. "Lucy, well, she's special. And we like you a lot, or we wouldn't be saying this. This is serious stuff. She's new around here and we noticed she doesn't date. She's too young to be sitting at home all the time."

"Hold it. You guys have been listening to Nana."

"True," Tony agreed. "But still. You know you like her and she deserves to go out on a real date. And you used to be gone all the time on dates and you never go now. So it'd be good for both of you."

Rowdy wanted to deny it all, but, truth was, taking Lucy on a date was a great idea.

"You ain't chicken, are you?" B.J. asked.

"No, Short Stuff, I am not chicken."

Tony and the other boys started high-fiving each other and Tony reached across the horse, holding his hand up. Rowdy gave him a high five.

It occurred to him later that the little sneaks had become proficient at getting adults to fall right into their traps.

First Lucy with the cow milking, and now him.

He chuckled, thinking about what easy prey he'd been.

Now the hard part. Getting Lucy to agree.

The smart thing would be to let the boys do their magic.

But this was *his* date. And he'd do the asking.

He just hoped Lucy didn't do the rejecting.

This was heaven on earth. It truly was. Lucy sat on her stool in front of her canvas in the center of her new studio with the awesome light shining through the windows. The painting had come at her fast and furious. Two days she'd been at it almost nonstop. That was how it was with her. When inspiration struck, there was no stopping it. She had to get it out onto the canvas.

Stepping away, she picked up her coffee and walked to the wide windows that overlooked her valley. Her sweet uncle. How had he known this place would be so perfect for her?

Turning back, she stared at the canvas. It was a

scene of the calf branding. The colors were vivid, bold. And though there were many in the picture, she hadn't been able to help herself—Rowdy was there, bent on one knee with his hand on B.J.'s shoulder, as the focal point. His features lit up the canvas—the softness in his eyes, the generous spirit coming full force to the scene was what would draw every eye to him. Just like it did in real life.

Lucy wasn't one to brag about her work. There had been a time when she brushed off compliments. But her agent had been the one who pointed out that her ability was a God-given talent and when she belittled it, she was telling God He hadn't done well by her.

Now she recognized it for what it was. And she thanked Him for blessing her with the ability.

Times like this, though, when she looked at a painting and recognized that she couldn't have done it without God's hand on her shoulder, were the moments that she was awestruck. She had feared to never feel that again.

She'd read an interview with an author once who said that there were times when the author would read something she wrote and she would go back and double-check her original manuscript thinking that an editor had switched the words because she couldn't remember writing something so profound. The author would be shocked when she'd realize she had indeed written the words and knew that God had given her the words.

That was how Lucy felt now.

"Lucy."

Rowdy! Like a deer in the headlights, she stared at

her painting and then at the stairs. The door was open and his spurs clinked with each step up the stairs.

He'd wanted to see her work. But she hadn't meant for a picture of himself to be the first thing of hers that he saw.

Frantically she set her coffee down and was about to grab the painting and do what? Throw it in the closet?

"Hey," he said, before she could do anything.

"Hey," she said, moving in front of the painting. Like he wasn't going to see the three-foot-by-four-foot canvas behind her.

He looked around appreciatively. "This is great, Lucy."

She couldn't help but smile. The room was long, the walls painted a fresh yellow, the color that inspired her. His attention was snagged by the large painting hanging on the wall closest to him. It was one of her rather stormy days, darker than usual and yet there was something about it that still appealed to Lucy. Most of the others hanging were not her usual signature style. On the wall at the end of the building was the single painting that she had from her days before the fire. It was a pale blue sky with two vivid bluebirds playing chase between the trees as a road curved past the tree and around the bend.

It was to that painting that Rowdy moved. "This is beautiful," he said.

His praise touched her. She moved over beside him and crossed her arms as she looked at the painting. "I painted that years ago—one of my first that I felt was saleable. I gave it to my dad—told him the bluebirds in the picture were to signify bluebirds of happiness. All the joy I wished for him in his life. After the fire, he and my new stepmother brought the painting to me during my recovery and said they wanted me to have it so that the bluebirds would remind me that I would be happy again."

She felt very self-conscious when Rowdy turned to look at her. There was no denying that she had feelings for Rowdy. Lucy had known as she painted him that, though she didn't want to face it, she was falling in love with him. And she didn't know what to do about it.

"You are, aren't you? Happy again?"

Oh, what a loaded question. She nodded. "I am, Rowdy. I have my hang-ups. But I am. And much of that is because of being here." She wanted to say *because of you* but she couldn't. She was confused about her emotions where he was concerned. And yet she knew that if she just released the fear holding her back and gave him a chance...

Her thoughts stalled as he reached suddenly and lifted a strand of hair from her shoulder and rubbed it between his fingers, studying it as if it held the secrets of the universe.

Had he almost touched her cheek? Longing for his touch further confused her.

His eyes met hers, and she prayed he couldn't read the longing in them. His lips curved into a smile. "I'm glad," he said, and let go of her hair.

"Is there a reason you came by?" she asked, wishing her voice didn't sound so breathless. But goodness, the room seemed twenty degrees hotter than it had and her cheeks were burning.

He strode back to the center of the room and the painting she'd been working on. It happened so quickly that she was still standing with her feet anchored to where she stood. From her position she couldn't see the painting, only his face as he viewed it. He studied the painting intently. And then he raised his eyes and looked at her over the top of the canvas.

"This is unbelievable."

The warm rush of satisfaction filled her. "I was inspired."

She didn't say by him. She hoped he didn't realize that he was the focal point of the painting.

"You put me in this painting."

"Yes." She decided to play it cool. "What was going on between you and B.J. in the photo captivated me. I couldn't help myself. You're very paintable." There, she'd taken the personal emphasis off of it and put it in professional terms. He looked back at the painting and she wished she knew what was going through his mind.

"B.J. and the boys will be blown away like I am."

She smiled broadly. "I do love to blow people away. I want them to feel loved, though." The words were out before she could stop them.

"I think they will."

He'd said it casually, not seeming to take her words to mean she wanted him to feel loved, too. And that was a good thing. Right? She didn't want to mislead him. Didn't want him to think she was playing games with him.

He dragged his hat from his head and tugged at his ear as she'd seen him do a few times.

"Okay, time for me to come clean. I came over here because I wanted to see if you'd have dinner and maybe a movie with me this weekend?"

If he'd walked over and kissed her she wouldn't have been more surprised.

"You're asking me on a date?"

He nodded, still holding his hat. She noticed he had a death grip on it, and that simple knowledge got her right in the center of her heart.

"But I—"

"Look, Lucy. Truthfully. I'm just going to lay it out here for you. I don't want to scare you. But I—I care for you. I'm trying to do everything you ask of me, and that includes keeping my distance, but I know that you know in your heart there is something between us. And I'm just asking for a chance. I know I've royally messed up in my past. And I've asked God to forgive me. All I'm asking is for you to give this connection we have a fighting chance."

Her hand came up and she toyed with the collar of her shirt. She was unable to speak or think past the reasons bombarding her that this was a terrible idea. She didn't want to do it. She didn't want to risk her heart. But she knew in her heart of hearts that she wanted so much to give "them" a chance. He'd messed up. But he had respected every boundary she'd put up since the kiss. Didn't he deserve something from her?

"Okay. I would like that."

Chapter Eighteen

"So I hear you have a date."

Lucy blinked in disbelief at Ms. Jo as she dabbed paint on the canvas. This was their first official Gals Night Out Paint Class, as they'd officially called it, and to her surprise she had over half a dozen students. Including Mabel, Ms. Jo, Nana and Jolie. The other three ladies were friends of theirs and just as chatty as they could be. Despite the fact that everything wasn't completely set up, they'd decided to get together anyway.

And it had been a fun night.

They'd had refreshments and she'd walked them through painting their first still life—a beautiful bunch of grapes she'd set on a platter and focused a spotlight on so that there would be shadows and highlights.

No one was painting masterpieces yet, but they were having a great time and Lucy had actually been happy that for a little while she was being distracted from the fact that she'd accepted a date with Rowdy for the next evening.

And now Ms. Jo had just opened her love life up

for group discussion. An internal groan threatened to burst out of her and expose her real fear.

"Yes, I am." She managed to sound calm. Amazing since she was a little bit freaked out about the whole thing.

"Jo, you weren't supposed to say anything about that," Mabel said. It was an odd turnaround that Mabel was getting onto Jo, when it was usually Ms. Jo keeping Mabel in line. "Ruby Ann shared that with us in strictest confidentiality."

Ms. Jo dipped her chin and looked over the rim of her glasses. "It's all over town, Mabel, in case you haven't noticed. I've been sitting here debating if she should be forewarned and decided that yes, it is our duty to let her know."

Nana looked worried. "It wasn't meant to get out. The boys ganged up on Rowdy and gave him the push he needed to ask you out. They convinced him it was the thing to do."

He'd asked her out because the boys talked him into it.

"Now, don't even start thinking he asked you out because the boys wanted him to." Jolie read her mind. "You know as well as all of us that he's been dying to ask you out, but wasn't sure it was the thing to do."

"Well, I heard Drewbaker and Chili discussing it on the bench out by the newspaper office," Vergie Little said, waving her brush.

Sissy Jackson and Bea Norton nodded their heads.

So everybody knew she was going on a date. The room burst into chatter about how nice it was and that she needed a night out and that Rowdy was a changed man.

Jolie didn't say much and Lucy said less. What else was there to say?

If she wanted to, she knew she could use this as an excuse not to go out with Rowdy. She could claim that he shouldn't have told everyone. Different reasons for calling off the date made themselves known to her as she listened to the gals cheer that she was finally going to have a night out like a young woman should.

And the truth was, she agreed. She could let Tim cause her to become a hermit or she could step out and force herself to have a life.

She was not a chicken.

Never had been and never would be. She wouldn't let herself.

And though she'd forgotten it for a while, that meant she had to fight the fear about going out with Rowdy.

She had to fight, to back it down or, like Mabel had reminded her again, the regrets would be hard to live with.

Rowdy deserved for her to give this a chance. Scars and all.

On Saturday evening at six o'clock Rowdy stood outside Lucy's back door, a bouquet of fresh spring flowers gripped in his hand. It had taken him almost thirty minutes at the florist to decide which to buy. He'd wanted all of them but knew that would be a little crazy. But that was how he felt about Lucy.

Rubbing the back of his neck, he took a deep breath and knocked on the door. He hoped she hadn't been looking out a window and saw how nervous he was. He had to be calm, cool and cautious. He could not mess this up.

But ever since he'd realized she'd painted his likeness on that canvas with such detail that even the emotion in his eyes had shown, he knew that Lucy Calvert was not only the most talented artist he'd ever seen, but she also just might care for him deep down. That scared her, and with good reason.

He'd prayed long and hard and he knew that the outcome of this night could very well be the most important of his life.

The door opened and he almost dropped the flowers. "Wow."

She took his breath away. For the first time since he'd known her she didn't have a work shirt on. Though she did have a long-sleeved blouse, it was shimmery silky material in a rich gold tone and she had a colorful scarf draped about her neck. She had hidden her scars without resorting to a bulky work shirt. She had skinny jeans on with strappy high-heeled sandals. She was at least five-two in the heels and it made him smile.

"You look gorgeous," he added to the *wow* he'd blurted out in pure reaction.

She bit her lip then smiled almost shyly. "Thank you. You, too— I mean, not gorgeous—handsome."

They both laughed and his nerves eased with the laughter.

"These are for you." He held the flowers out to her and she took them almost eagerly.

"How lovely. You shouldn't have," she said, but he could tell that he'd chosen right. And that she was pleased.

"Come in, let me put these in water and then I'm ready."

He followed her into the kitchen and watched as she

filled a vase from a cupboard, then arranged the flowers, taking time to make them look great. It was amazing what a difference she could make just by pushing and pulling a few flowers here and there. The artist in her was evident in more than her painting.

"Okay," she said, turning to him. "They are beautiful and I'm ready."

But was he? Praying he wouldn't mess up, he held the door for her and they were soon on their way.

It was a lovely evening. The sun was just beginning to set when Rowdy opened the door of his truck for her. He held out his hand and the fiery orange sky lit the world behind him as Lucy took his hand. It felt as explosive as her emotions. His eyes were dark with what she thought was worry. She'd been watching for his arrival. How could she not, with her nerves jingling like they were? And she hadn't missed the hesitancy in his posture and the anxious expression on his face as he'd knocked on the door. He'd been tense since she opened it…other than when he'd almost made her blush by his appreciative appraisal when he first saw her.

He was as uptight about the date as she was.

"I'd better hold on tight or you might topple off those heels of yours," he said, squeezing her fingers gently and eyeing her sandals.

There he was, her happy-go-lucky guy.

Her guy?

"I haven't had any reason to wear heels since I've been here," she said with a smile, suddenly feeling a small semblance of ease between them. "But I'm quite steady on my feet in them."

"Too bad," he said, still holding her hand as he

placed his hand on her waist to help her as she stepped up into his truck. "I was hoping you'd need my assistance all evening."

Her heart was fluttering as she sat in the seat, eye level with him and so very near. "I'll probably need it. After saying that I'll probably twist my ankle or something."

"Not on my watch, sweetheart." He tugged her seat belt out and stretched it around her and clamped it in place, meeting her gaze as he leaned over her. "You're safe with me. Heels or no heels."

She could not breathe as he withdrew, closed her door and strode around to slide into the driver's seat. Yup, that sunset didn't even compare to the intense emotions at war inside her as he pulled out onto the blacktop and headed toward wherever.... She didn't even know where they were going and she didn't care. Tonight she felt alive, and beautiful in his eyes—she wasn't allowing herself to think about her scars. Not tonight. Tonight she was a regular woman on a regular date.

Yet she took that back as she looked over at Rowdy's profile. This could never be considered a regular date. Nothing with Rowdy could ever be considered regular. He was special and she knew it.

Rowdy had seriously contemplated where to take Lucy to dinner. It had to be nice. It had to make her feel as special as he thought she was and it had to be romantic. He was going to make sure she knew this wasn't just two friends going out for a burger.

He finally decided on a little Greek place off the beaten path in River Bend. After the hour it took to reach the larger town, they'd both relaxed a little and were talking and laughing about the antics of the boys. The boys were always a safe subject.

The hostess seated them in a quiet corner of the restaurant at a table for two. Soft music played in the background, candles flickered at tables in the dim light. Lucy's smile of appreciation was all he needed to know he'd chosen right.

"This is nice. I love the atmosphere." She talked about the unique color of deep green on the walls, how the rich hardwood floors combined with it and about the chandeliers hanging overhead made from tree branches. "I think they were going for romance in the outdoors," she said softly. "It's really a neat place, though descriptions would never do it justice."

He chuckled. "You've done a good job. I like the atmosphere, but the food is excellent."

"I would have never taken you for a guy who would eat anything other than steak. Greek. Who would have thought it?"

"Hey, that's stereotyping. Cowboys enjoy things other than steak and potatoes."

"So I see. And I like that very much."

By the time their meal had come and they'd nearly finished, he and Lucy were having a good time. Lucy's eyes sparkled in the candlelight and she'd even flirted with him a few times. It hit him full force that this was who she'd been before her husband had stolen her ability to trust.

When she laughed at something he said about the boys ganging up on him to give him the courage to ask her out, he couldn't help reaching across and tracing the back of her hand with his fingers.

"I'm so glad they convinced me to see if you would accept a date with me," he said, turning serious. "I'd convinced myself there wasn't a chance."

She flipped her hand over so that she was holding his hand. "I still can't believe I said yes. I am so glad I came."

As she said the words that reached inside him like warmth from a flame, she looked up, distracted. He turned his head to see if the waitress had come back with their check, but his heart went cold when he saw Liz approaching, her gaze locked on him like a target at a shooting range.

Chapter Nineteen

"Rowdy, I saw those amazing shoulders of yours and that black hair and knew instantly it was you."

Lucy had known the woman was coming their way on purpose. Even the distraction of Rowdy's hand holding hers hadn't prevented her from seeing the way this woman zeroed in on Rowdy. She was an amazing creature—tall, willowy, with hair so blond and so shiny it caught every flicker of light as it framed one of the most beautiful faces Lucy had ever seen.

She'd yet to look at Lucy and had eyes for only Rowdy, who, Lucy noted as he'd drawn his hand from hers, looked a little pale beneath his tan. His eyes had darkened with—anger or appreciation? She wasn't sure. But though he didn't say anything, she felt the tension in him even across the table.

The beautiful woman gave a sultry pout that Lucy figured a man might find attractive. She herself would look silly even trying such a move. Lucy decided with a quick judgment that she didn't like this woman.

Something curled inside Lucy as the woman's predatory gaze flickered over Rowdy. At the calculated way she flicked a strand of champagne-colored hair from her shoulder. Even the way she stood was a pose to bring attention to her figure as she crowded Rowdy's personal space.

"I've missed you," she said, perfect hands toying with the silk tie at the low neckline of her blouse.

Lucy sat very still, her gaze shifting to Rowdy. Why was he not saying anything? His gaze was locked on the woman and a muscle in his check flinched.

"I have nothing to say to you, Liz," he said at last.

Liz, as he'd called her, gave a soft laugh. "Not so fast, handsome. You need to know I'm divorcing Garret. So no more of that messy situation. I'm a free agent and I'd love to see you sometime. You have my number."

The moment she realized who this was, Lucy went cold inside. Liz turned and walked away, letting her hand slide casually to her back pocket—another calculated move to draw attention as she strolled away. Rowdy didn't watch her leave; instead, he was looking straight at Lucy.

Despite the anxious way Rowdy was eyeing her, she couldn't speak. So many things were running through her mind. This was the kind of woman he'd dated. This was the married woman he'd had the affair with. What a horrible creature she was, and this was the woman— the *type* of woman—that Rowdy had found attractive.

She was beautiful, but— "I'm ready to leave," Lucy said, barely able to look at Rowdy.

He motioned for the waitress, who quickly brought them their check, and within minutes they were out the door and in the truck. It couldn't have been fast enough for Lucy. Her stomach churned and she was almost afraid she was going to be ill.

What had she been thinking? How had she let herself fall into this pit?

Rowdy didn't say much. He was, it seemed, as upset as she was. Halfway home he pulled off the road into someone's pasture entrance and put the truck in Park.

Rubbing the crease that had formed across his forehead, he sighed. "That couldn't have gone more wrong if I'd have written it in a book. Lucy, I know you've got all kinds of bad things going on inside your head right now. I'm sorry that happened. But I'm more sorry I ever got involved with her."

Lucy looked out the window into the darkness. What could she say?

"Talk to me, Lucy."

"About what?" she snapped. Anger that had been coiled inside of her broke loose. "I should never have let this happen. I should never have let my guard down."

"Lucy, I'm not the same stupid guy I used to be. I'm not."

She turned toward him. "It doesn't matter. Don't you see I can't do this—us? *I* can't do this. Please take me home."

Rowdy had died and *not* gone to heaven. That was for certain.

Tucker and Morgan had come out to his house, a small place that he'd taken over after he'd moved out of the big house. It was hidden in the woods, and it worked as a great place to hole up when he wanted to be alone.

And he wanted to be alone.

"What's going on?" Tucker asked, finding him on the back porch where he'd been nursing a strong cup of coffee and a sour mood.

"Now, why would you think there was anything wrong?" he asked, sarcasm thick as the yaupon growing in the woods around them.

Morgan shot him a concerned look. "You didn't show up at church Sunday or work yesterday. And Jolie said that when Lucy came to teach art, she looked about as gloomy as a stormy night."

"The boys noticed, too, and kept asking her how your date went," Tucker added. Even the fact that his brother had driven out here said he was worried, and Rowdy knew it. How many times had his brothers had to come get him out of trouble when he was growing up?

"Oh, yeah, and what did she say when they asked her that?" He had his elbows on his knees and was studying the planks between his boots.

"She told them it went fine. But no one believes her."

"She's not doing fine," he muttered. "I messed up and made her feel bad." Sitting up, he looked at his brothers. He'd never felt as terrible and low as he felt now. He'd spent time praying and venting and wishing he'd taken back ever pushing Lucy to go out with him. And he said as much to his brothers. "Her lousy husband left her with a tremendous amount of emotional scar tissue. The last thing she needed was a man like me thinking there was anything but heartache that I could offer her."

Morgan placed his hand on his shoulder. "Rowdy, you don't need to be talking like that. You have a lot to offer Lucy, or any woman, for that matter. You've made some mistakes, but who of us hasn't one way or the other? You've changed."

"Yes, I have, but I'm no good for Lucy. Lucy needs

a man who has been a rock from day one. A solid man she knows she can trust."

Tucker pulled up a chair and sat across from him, looking him square in the eye. "It's not for you to say what kind of man she needs. God knows the man she needs and as far as I can tell He's put you in her life. Now, whether He's put you in her life to be the man she's to end up with, I can't say, brother. But I can tell you that He didn't put you in her life by accident."

Rowdy grunted cynically. But Lucy falling out of the hayloft and into his arms flashed across his mind.

Tucker ignored him. "What you're going through right now is going to come into play one way or another. What I want to know is, are you committed to see it through? When I was in Iraq I didn't need men beside me who were in halfway. I needed commitment even though we had no idea what the outcome was going to be. Do you love her?"

Morgan yanked a chair up and crossed his arms. His hiked brow posed the same question.

Rowdy nodded slowly, mulling over what Tucker had said. Tucker wasn't a man of a lot of words. Rowdy set his coffee on the side table and sat up. "I do," he said aloud. He'd made a commitment to God that he was going to wait for his direction in his life. He'd made more mistakes along the way where Lucy was concerned, but she hadn't just dropped in his arms for nothing.

Rowdy was certain of that.

"Then the question is, are you going to see this through, wherever it goes, even if it's not in your favor?" Morgan finally spoke and Tucker nodded as he talked.

"I've been so caught up in the fact that I wasn't right for Lucy that I never even stopped to consider if God had a different reason for me being here for her." His mind was suddenly churning. He told his brothers about Liz showing up and how it had affected Lucy.

"She barely spoke to me after that. And just wanted to go home. Then she told me she couldn't see me anymore."

"And you gave up, just like that?" Tucker asked. "That's not the guy I know."

"Hey, I changed, remember?"

Morgan shook his head. "Rowdy, just because you changed doesn't mean you roll over and play dead. God's not going to do all the work, you know."

Rowdy scowled at his brothers. "Hey, why are y'all still here, anyway? I've got somewhere to be." He stood up and strode through the house and straight to his truck.

"It's about time," Tucker called after him.

And Morgan's, "We'll be praying for you both," was the last thing he heard before he slammed his truck door closed and revved his engine.

It was time to see his girl....

Lucy couldn't help but worry that she'd hurt Rowdy. She'd been so upset after the date that she'd not said much, and she'd left him in her driveway in a very unkind way.

Just as he had done from the moment she'd told him about Tim and her burns, he'd again done as she wished. He'd not tried to kiss her and he'd kept his hands to himself. He'd been nothing but kind to her.

And all that he'd asked of her was to give this, this *thing* between them a chance.

And then this Liz person showed up and made her... what? Jealous? Feel inferior in a physical way?

Liz, as horrible as she was and as much a soul that Lucy knew needed the Lord in her life, had shown Lucy that Rowdy deserved so much more than either she or Liz could offer him.

By Tuesday morning Lucy knew she had to talk to Rowdy. Pulling up to the ranch, she looked around for Rowdy's truck but she didn't see it. She learned from Jolie and the kids on Monday during afternoon art class that no one had seen him on Sunday and he hadn't shown up at the main ranch compound at all on Monday.

Lucy hadn't shown up for church on Sunday, either, and felt guilty about that, but she had been too upset.

As she looked around now, her spirits plummeted further because she'd felt compelled to talk to him. Not feeling like seeing anyone else, she turned her truck around in the parking lot and headed back home. In her rearview mirror, she caught a glimpse of Tony coming out of the barn, leading his horse. But she didn't stop. She was in no shape to talk to anyone right now. Except Rowdy.

Once she made it back to her house, she slammed out of her truck and walked to the barn. She pulled open the double doors and didn't bother to close them behind her. Her boots clattered on the steps as she jogged up to her studio. She had every intention of trying to paint, but Rowdy stared back at her from his painting and all she could do was stand there and stare back.

She loved him.

It was as clear in the painting as anything she'd ever known in her heart. She'd painted the picture with love and she hadn't even recognized it until now.

Closing her eyes, she let the realization pour over her and she tried to absorb what it meant for her. Nothing.

How long she stood there she wasn't sure, but she tried in every way to convince herself that her falling in love with Rowdy was a blessing sent from God to help her heal. But it wasn't, and there was no use trying to convince herself of the fact.

"Lucy, are you up there?"

Rowdy!

Her heart jumped into her throat and she panicked. He was here! "Yes," she said, stilling herself for a very hard conversation. But it was one that needed to be started and finished. She would not walk away from this again. Rowdy deserved to know her heart.

His steps were quick as he, too, jogged up the stairs. She was startled when she saw him. He hadn't shaved and a five-o'clock shadow roughened his jaw. He stopped inside the doorway for the first few seconds. Lucy fought the need to wrap her arms around him and tell him she was so sorry.

To tell him that she trusted him and that she knew he was a changed man. That everything he'd shown her of his character had been that of a man of integrity.

"Lucy, I've come to say my piece." He crossed to stand just a step away from her. "You're a stubborn woman. And I've realized that I've been letting you have your way just a little too much."

What?

"I'm a changed man. I have messed up and messed up some more and I'll mess up in the future, I can promise you that. But I can promise you that if I give you my word about anything—and I mean anything— I'll come through with it. I'll never lie or cheat on you. I've never done that with anyone, even before I made a commitment to God that I was changing the way I lived. So you can rest assured that with a good woman like you—the woman I love—that I'd be a man of integrity till my dying breath."

Lucy's temper had spiked at the high-handed way he'd started off, but that anger had diffused like a popped balloon.

"I believe you," she said. And it was so true. "You are not Tim. Tim was never the man you are and I've come to realize that as I thought about this for the past few days."

He'd said he loved her.

Lucy closed her eyes and let the bittersweet knowledge seep into the dark places of her heart. Tears threatened and she backed them into a corner knowing this was not the time to cry *or* to be weak. And it was most positively not the time to be selfish.

Touching his cheek, she smiled at him. "I treated you badly, Rowdy. So badly, and I am so very sorry for that. You are so special. But you have this all wrong. I was upset the other night because…" She couldn't tell him she was jealous. "Because I realized when I looked at Liz that you deserve so much more. More than she or I could give you."

His brows met and his head cocked as if in question. He started to speak and she shook her head.

"Please, I need to finish." She pulled her hand away and took a deep breath. "When I said I couldn't do this, I was saying that *I* can't. Not because of anything you've done. I just can't do it. Beneath this shirt is a body so scarred that even I have a hard time looking at it. I don't have it in me to share. As a wife, I'd feel so inferior."

"Don't talk that way," he snapped, letting his eyes fall to her work shirt. "I don't care what your body looks like. Lucy, I love you. The fact that you have scars doesn't matter to me. They would only remind me of the strength and courage you've shown in the face of great adversity. You are beautiful to me, mind, body and soul."

She hardened her heart against what he was saying. She refused to let her guard down. "No, Rowdy. I'm damaged beyond repair in my mind and I can't—" A crash downstairs halted her words. Rowdy spun around and started for the stairs just as the nicker of a horse sounded and then hooves pounded on hard ground.

Running to the window, Lucy felt sick when she saw Tony galloping across the pasture like wolves were chasing him.

"Rowdy, it's Tony. He must have heard what I said."

"Come on." She raced down the stairs and didn't ask questions as she jumped into his truck. She held on as he backed out of the driveway as if they'd been shot out of a cannon.

"Where will he go?"

Rowdy didn't say anything. He turned into a drive a few yards down the road that led into a pasture of the

Sunrise Ranch and drove over the cattle guard and into
the pasture that stretched between her house and the
ranch. Lucy studied his profile as they bounced over
that rutted gravel road. They hadn't gone far when he
detoured to another road and spun gravel, fishtailing
to make the direction change. He was angry.

Everything about him radiated anger as they charged
over the pasture in pursuit of Tony.

All she could think about were the scars on Tony's
body. And the pain her words must have caused him.

She started praying. In the distance she glimpsed
him, riding low as he and the horse practically flew
up one hill and disappeared over the other. In the distance she could see the stable.

"He's going home."

"Yes. He's going to the stable," Rowdy said tersely,
sounding as though he'd known exactly where Tony
would go. "The place he feels safe."

Lucy snapped her head to stare at Rowdy. His curt
words had been matter-of-fact. "How do you know
that?"

"When he first came to us, that was where we'd
find him when things got too hard for him to handle.
He'll go into a stall."

When they reached the yard, Lucy was shocked to
see the boys climbing out of the arena with looks of
concern and curiosity on their faces as they headed
toward the stable. Tony's horse was standing alone at
the entrance, breathing hard. But Tony was nowhere
to be seen.

Rowdy bailed out of the truck in an instant and she
followed.

"Stop, guys. Let me go in by myself," he commanded Wes and Joseph, who were almost at the entrance but had stopped when they saw Rowdy.

"He was flying when he rounded the arena and charged through here," Joseph said.

"Flying," Wes echoed, spitting a sunflower seed. "What's wrong with him, Rowdy?"

Lucy walked past them without answering. "Let me, Rowdy. I did this. I need to fix it." Without waiting, she walked into the barn and started down the center of the alley. About halfway down she saw a stall gate slightly ajar. Tugging it open, she stepped inside. Tony was sitting in the corner—his knees drawn up and his arms folded over them with his head down.

After all the pain this kid had suffered, she'd just caused him more. It was unbearable to her. Foolish, foolish woman.

Swallowing the lump in her throat and praying for the right words—something she'd been sorely lacking of late—she sank down beside him in the soft hay. "Tony. I'm sorry."

"It's nothing but the truth," he said, not looking up. He swiped his face on his shirtsleeve. "I came to tell you that I met a girl." His words were muffled against his arm.

Normally for a kid of fifteen, this would be no big deal, but Tony didn't talk to girls much. He was shy around them and she knew exactly why, just as most of the fellas did. His burns.

"I think that's wonderful," she said, but he shook his head. "I know you worry about your scars."

His head shot up and he glared at her. "I heard what you told Rowdy."

Shame suffused Lucy. *I'm damaged beyond repair*

in my mind and I can't— "I was so afraid," she said, aching inside with regret. "Oh, Tony. It's complicated."

"Yeah, it's easy to tell me one thing and believe another. You made me believe God would have a woman out there when I grow up. And for her my scars wouldn't matter."

"Everything she said is true," Rowdy said, entering the stall. "There will be someone out there who won't care. Who will love you with all their heart."

He was talking to Tony, but Lucy knew he was also telling her.

"But the key will be whether you love that woman back. Because that's going to be the tough part, Tony. You'll have to love that person, too, because even if she doesn't have physical scars, she'll have warts of some kind. We all do. She'll have messed up. She won't be perfect. But if you love her enough to trust her with your heart and your scars, and to trust what God has done for you, then you have nothing to worry about."

Tony was looking from Rowdy to Lucy.

"Is that how you feel about Lucy?"

Rowdy gave him a smile that melted her chilled, ashamed heart. He nodded. "I love Lucy, scars and all. Especially with her scars. But the question is, how does she feel about me?"

Tony and Rowdy were both looking at her.

"Don't let your scars stop you, Lucy," Tony said, trying to give her courage. "Do you love him?"

Lucy nodded. How could she not after everything he'd just said? "I do love you, Rowdy."

The words were soft, but they were sure. She held her hand up, and he took it and tugged her to her feet.

"Can you trust me with your heart and your scars? And to love you always?"

She knew she could. "Yes. I already do."

A to-die-for smile flashed across his face and he pulled her into his arms—a sense of home sweet home swept through her at the ironclad strength that wrapped around her.

"Then you'll marry me?" he asked, looking deep into her eyes.

"Yes. Oh, yes, I will," she said, and with the words her heart opened wide. Tony scrambled to his feet behind them and raced from the stall.

"They're gettin' *married!*" he shouted gleefully as he went.

Lucy laughed. "He's going to be okay."

"And so are we," Rowdy said. "You asked me not to kiss you again. But do you think you could make an exception and I could kiss you this once?"

Oh, how she loved this man. Touching his cheek with her palm, she drew his head toward her. "Would you kiss me forever, please?"

And that was all the encouragement he needed as Rowdy's lips met hers with a sigh. "I thought you'd never ask."

"Hubba, hubba! That's what I'm talking about," Wes said, and Lucy and Rowdy jerked apart to find all the boys crammed against the stall railing, peering at them. "Hey, don't stop on our account," the teen said, holding up a hand. "Come on, fellas, let's give these two lovebirds some space."

And with that, sixteen smiling faces backed up and followed their leader out of the barn.

"Now, where were we?" Rowdy asked, his eyes

twinkling as he slipped an arm beneath her knees and swung her up and into his arms.

Lucy wrapped her arms around his neck. "Right where I've belonged from the first moment I met you," she said.

"There you go, talking some sense now," Rowdy chuckled, and kissed her again....

* * * * *

Dear Reader,

I'm so very thrilled that you joined me for *Her Unexpected Cowboy,* book two of my new Cowboys of Sunrise Ranch series! I hope you enjoyed your visit with the McDermotts and all the boys on the ranch and their friends in Dew Drop, Texas.

This book was very special to me because it deals with the scars, both emotional and physical, that Rowdy and Lucy were dealing with in their lives. I believe we all have scars of some kind, and they are challenging to come to terms with sometimes.

I was compelled by Rowdy's challenge to change his life. This is a challenge many face, and their strength, conviction, courage and inspiration to do so inspired me to write this story. I pray that if you have committed your life to the Lord and are looking to make a change, that you trust the Lord, focus on Him and take His lead in your new path. Pray that He will guide your steps and put people in your path who will help and encourage you. Realize, too, that sometimes changing means leaving some friends behind and building new and healthy relationships. Building a personal relationship with Jesus Christ is the relationship that matters the most.

I love to hear from readers. You can reach me in any manner of ways! You can find me on Facebook at facebook.com/debra.clopton.5, Twitter @debraclopton, and Goodreads, too.

My website is www.debraclopton.com. Or if you prefer good old snail mail, you can reach me at Debra Clopton, P.O. Box 1125, Madisonville, Texas 77864.

God bless you in all you do!

Until next time, live, laugh and seek God with all your hearts!

Debra Clopton

Questions for Discussion

1. Rowdy had made a life-changing decision when we first met him. Why did he make this decision?

2. Lucy had lived through not one, but two life-changing experiences when we first met her. What were they?

3. Lucy and Rowdy met when she literally fell into his arms. Neither one of them was looking for a romance, but they felt the instant attraction that sparked between them. Have you ever had a life-changing opportunity that arrived in God's timing and not yours? How did you handle it?

4. Lucy was still dealing with the emotional scars left over from her husband's betrayal. The remodeling of her home was cathartic to her—she found she loved knocking out walls. When you are feeling blue, do you believe physical release can help you better than sitting and worrying?

5. Tony believed no one would ever love him because of his scars. How did his friends help him? How did he help Lucy?

6. When Rowdy began to fall in love with Lucy, it was confusing to him because he had vowed not to begin a relationship for a year, as he waited to meet the woman God chose for him. But he was strongly tempted to break his vow. Has something

like this ever happened to you in any area of your life? How did you deal with it?

7. Rowdy was trying to leave his checkered past behind him and live a better life. But it seemed that Lucy saw his imperfections and instantly didn't trust him. Why do you think her view of him mattered almost instantly to Rowdy?

8. As with Rowdy, when someone commits to changing their life and reforming their lifestyle, is it an easy thing? Sometimes living down your past is the hardest thing of all, but setting goals and seeking friend and family support is a good thing. Who were Rowdy's supporters?

9. How did Lucy hurt Tony? Tony said it was easy to tell someone else how to accept themselves, but it wasn't so easy to do if it's you who needs to accept the scars. Did Lucy realize she wasn't trusting God like she thought she was?

10. Did it take courage for Tony, Rowdy and Lucy to all deal with their scars? Do you have the courage you need to deal with your scars?

COMING NEXT MONTH FROM
Love Inspired®

Available January 21, 2014

THE COWBOY'S REUNITED FAMILY
Cooper Creek
Brenda Minton

When the wife and daughter Blake Cooper's been searching for suddenly show up in town, can he learn to forgive, and save his family?

UNEXPECTED FATHER
Hearts of Hartley Creek
Carolyne Aarsen

Rancher Denny Norquest has a plan, and it doesn't include the baby on his doorstep. Evangeline Arsenau's offered to help—but the beauty next door could prove to be a bigger distraction to the future he's mapped out.

THE FOREST RANGER'S RETURN
Leigh Bale

Dal Savatch has given up on romance. But when the injured war hero is reunited with his high school sweetheart, he'll have to prove to her—and himself—that they're meant to be together forever.

HER VALENTINE SHERIFF
Serendipity Sweethearts
Deb Kastner

Deputy Sheriff Eli Bishop won't let his fear of dogs stop him from leading the new K-9 unit. But after being left at the altar, he *is* afraid of opening his heart. Can trainer Mary Travis teach him to trust—and love—again?

MOMMY WANTED
Renee Andrews

She's made some mistakes in her past, but Kate Wydell is determined to set things right. Can she convince an entire town—and one special man— she's worthy of a second chance?

A DAUGHTER'S HOMECOMING
Ginny Aiken

Gaby Carlini returns home to rescue her family's pizza shop—but she can't do it alone. When former restaurateur Zach Davenport comes to her aid, love will soon be on the menu.

LICNM0114

REQUEST YOUR FREE BOOKS!

2 FREE INSPIRATIONAL NOVELS
PLUS 2
FREE
MYSTERY GIFTS

Love Inspired

SPECIAL EXCERPT FROM

Love Inspired

When the family he's been searching for finally returns,
Blake Cooper's not sure if he can ever forgive or forget.

Read on for a preview of
THE COWBOY'S REUNITED FAMILY
by Brenda Minton, Book #7 in the
COOPER CREEK series.

"I can't undo what I did." She leaned back against the wall
and with her fingers pinched the bridge of her nose. Soft
blond hair framed her face.

"No, you can't." He guessed he didn't need to tell her
what an understatement that was. She'd robbed him. She'd
robbed Lindsey. Come to think of it, she'd robbed his entire
family. Lindsey's family.

Jana's shoulder started to shake. Her body sagged against
the wall and her knees buckled. He grabbed her, holding her
close as she sobbed into his shoulder. She still fit perfectly
and he didn't want that. He didn't want to remember how it
had been when they were young. He didn't want her scent
to be familiar or her touch to be the touch he missed.

It all came back to him, holding her. He pushed it away
by remembering coming home to an empty house and a note.

He held her until her sobs became quieter, her body
ceased shaking. He held her and he tried hard not to think
about the years he'd spent searching, wishing things could
have been different for them, wishing she'd come back.

"Mrs. Cooper?"

He realized he was still holding Jana, his hands stroking
her hair, comforting her. His hands dropped to his sides and

she stepped back, visibly trying to regain her composure. She managed a shaky smile.

"She'll be fine," he assured the woman in the white lab coat, who was walking toward them, her gaze lingering on Jana.

"I'm Nurse Bonnie Palmer. If you could join me in the conference room, we'll discuss what needs to happen next for your daughter."

Jana shook her head. "I'm going to stay with Lindsey."

Blake gave her a strong look and pushed back a truckload of suspicion. She wasn't going anywhere with Lindsey. Not now. He knew that and he'd fight through the doubts about Jana and her motives. He'd do what he had to do to make sure Lindsey got the care she needed.

He'd deal with his ex-wife later.

He's committed to helping his daughter, but can Blake Cooper ever trust the wife who broke his heart?

Pick up THE COWBOY'S REUNITED FAMILY *to find out. Available February 2014 wherever Love Inspired® Books are sold.*